A

Alyssa Jefferson is ready to start her veterinary internship at the Rockin' K ranch, in the beautiful Colorado Rockies, where she will be assisting with the births of over three hundred pregnant cows. It's a dream come true, and she's so excited the joy is oozing from her. As icing on the cake, it appears the brothers that own the ranch are sexy as can be. A few months with some eye candy, is just what the doctor ordered.

Beau Kipling sees the sweet young thing coming for her riding lesson, and feels a kick to his gut. What is this hot young woman doing dating a man old enough to be her father? He's so ticked off, he can't stop himself from being an ass to her. He's never, in his whole life, felt the instant attraction he feels for this female, and she's some old guys arm candy.

When the truth is revealed, that Alyssa is his intern for the spring, and not the sheriff's new girlfriend, Beau knows he's blown it. And he can't even explain why he was so mean. No woman wants to hear a guy thought she was a gold digger. Now they must work together all spring. Can he convince her to give him a second chance?

A COWBOY FOR ALYSSA

SHIRLEY PENICK

∾

Photography: Tom Tyson

Cover Models: Shane Rice and Amanda Wilson

Cover design:Cassy Roop of Pink Ink Designs

Editing: Deelylah Mullin

Formatting: Cora Cade

Contact Shirley

www.shirleypenick.com

www.facebook.com/ShirleyPenickAuthor

To sign up for Shirley's New Release Newsletter, send email to shirleypenick@outlook.com, Subject: Newsletter.

ALSO BY SHIRLEY PENICK

LAKE CHELAN SERIES

The Rancher's Lady: A Lake Chelan novella

Hank & Ellen's story

Sawdust and Satin: Lake Chelan #1

Chris and Barbara's story

Designs on Her: Lake Chelan #2

Jeremy and Amber's story

COMING SOON

Fire on the Mountain: Lake Chelan #4

Trey and Mary Ann's story

∼

BURLAP AND BARBED WIRE SERIES

A Cowboy for Alyssa: Burlap and Barbed Wire #1

Beau and Alyssa's story

COMING SOON

Taming Adam: Burlap and Barbed Wire #2

Adam and Rachel's story

DEDICATION

To the cowboys and cowgirls from my own life. To the Penick family who are and were cattle ranchers in Wyoming and Nebraska. To my brother and sister and best friends who were Westernaires and where I learned to drive a horse trailer at the age of sixteen to get them to practice and events. To the Willis family who owned the feedstore and taught me the difference between hay and straw and much more. To the Nelson's ranch just inside the Rocky Mountain National Park where I spent many summers in the high country of Colorado. To country music and the National Western Stock Show and, of course, all the old John Wayne movies my dad loved to watch. This series comes from you all.

CHAPTER 1

*A*lyssa Jefferson turned her red Chevy Equinox into the driveway for the Rockin' K ranch, under the sign declaring it as such, and over the cattle grate. She was excited to start her spring internship as a veterinary assistant. The Colorado State University had hooked her up with this internship near the town of Spirit Lake in the beautiful Colorado Rockies for the second half of the spring semester, which was the last class that would complete her degree.

Her dad had tried to entice her to do her internship on his ranch, promising to let her play vet with their tiny herd, but she knew they would all pat her on the head and treat her like she was still eight years old, and not a senior in college, nearly finished with her bachelor's degree in biomedical science. Plus, it didn't seem fair to go back home for this last class. So, she'd told him that she would come home for summer after graduation. She could stay on at the Rockin' K through the summer if she wanted to, but summers were the slow season for veterinarians on a ranch. Most of the summer was spent fixing fences and growing hay for the winter. Until late July or early August when they would start breeding. Cattle ranches were always busy, but the work changed with the seasons.

She'd told the Kipling family she would be arriving today, but had not given them an exact time. She drove down the driveway and over a small bridge crossing over the top of a creek, definitely not the Colorado River, which had to run through their property somewhere. Once she'd crossed the creek and gotten past the trees she could see the house, it was a huge house, and not far from it was an even bigger barn, and a corral. Behind all of that was a gorgeous meadow with the Rockies in the background. The view was spectacular.

She turned into the parking area and got out of her car and stretched, deciding to leave her bags in the car until after she'd talked to someone from the family. She'd dressed up for her first meeting with them with her best jeans, a satin shirt, a leather fringed jacket, and her dress-up cowboy boots. The ones she wore for parties, instead of her working boots. Makeup and jewelry completed the look which was a rare occurrence for her. Alyssa had laughed at her reflection in the mirror this morning, thinking about the first time her third-grade teacher had come out to their home for a ride with the family. It had been her first date with Alyssa's widowed father and Ellen had dressed like Alyssa was dressed today, minus the jacket. Not at all practical for a ride or working on a ranch, but Alyssa was there to meet new people, so she felt it was appropriate attire for today.

A man came out of the barn, so she walked around the front of the car to greet him. Whoa, they grow them sexy here in Colorado—the guy is a hottie. He had black curly hair and blue eyes, and wore traditional cowboy garb of jeans and a chambray shirt that fit him to perfection, and showed every bit of his finely-tuned self. *This internship is going to be even better than I thought, with that eye candy running around.*

2

~

BEAU GROANED when he saw the woman come around the front of her red SUV. A city slicker for sure. No one in their right mind would come for their first riding lesson in a satin shirt, brand-new jeans, a leather jacket, and fancy hand tooled boots. She was going to be a hot mess after the lesson —he usually started a greenhorn with some grooming instructions. That way the rider became more familiar with the horse, before getting up on the animal. Especially the timid ones—and he'd been told this one was supposed to be scared to death. The town sheriff, Drake Carlson, had asked if they would teach his new girlfriend to ride, and they had agreed.

Great. How he'd drawn the short straw to teach this one he had no clue. She looked to be in her early twenties, and why someone that age was hooking up with a man in his fifties was beyond him. Sure, Drake was a nice guy and had plenty of cash to show a lady a good time, but he wasn't a millionaire or anything like that, so why was this sweet young thing with him? And why was Drake with her? He was usually much more sensible about his women.

None of his business—his job was to teach her that horses were not scary, and they were easy to ride. As long as you got a docile one, and he'd picked the perfect mare for her. He slapped his hat against his leg and walked over to the woman.

"Hello, welcome to the Rockin' K. I'm Beau Kipling."

"Hi, Beau. I'm Alyssa Jefferson." She smiled at him and every brain cell deserted him. He didn't hear another word she said. The woman was a knock out up close, and that smile was killer. She had green eyes that drew him in and a sweetheart mouth. Her brown hair was long, halfway to her waist and not curly, but not quite straight either. She finished talking and held out her hand to shake. He automatically took her hand in his and lightening shot through him at the touch. That just pissed him off, this gorgeous young thing was going out with a man over twice her age. He had never had this kind of reaction to a woman in his life, and she was taken by an old guy. Damn it all to hell. He wanted nothing to do with her and her riding lessons.

He sneered down at her clothes. "Those are pretty fancy clothes to be wearing out here on the ranch. I suppose you think you can dress like a princess and not get dirty. Horses are animals, and they get dirty. If you are going to be working with them and riding them, you can't be wearing satin and lace, princess."

Alyssa's cheeks flooded with color and she opened her mouth. "I know, I just—"

"Save it. Follow me." He glared at her and then started marching toward the barn. He pointed at the corral. "That is a corral, and this is a barn. The big scary horses are in the barn. It's where we stable them when they are not out in the pasture. I've got a nice old mare for you to ride that shouldn't scare your little self too much. But first, you are going to learn how to groom her."

"But I know—"

"Save it." He took a curry comb down off a peg and handed it to her. "This is a curry comb. It's kind of like a hair brush for horses. It helps to remove mud and other muck off the horse." Deciding to be a real jerk, he started handing her every grooming item he could find, piling them into her hands with a smart-ass comment on what they were for. He knew he was being an ass, but he just couldn't stop himself— he was too pissed off at her being some old man's arm candy.

When she couldn't hold one more item he took the hoof pick down and hung it on her little finger. "That's a hoof pick, you clean rocks and debris out of the horse's hoof with it."

"Beau, I think you've mistaken me—"

"Oh, no mistake about it, princess. I just don't like women who—"

Beau's younger brother, Chase, came into the barn, speaking before they could see him. "Beau, Drake just called and said he and Mary are running late and will be here in about a half hour." He rounded the corner and stopped and looked at them. Then he grinned, "You must be Alyssa. I'm Chase. Welcome to the Rockin' K, I'm glad you made it. Whatever are you doing holding every grooming tool we own?"

He started taking them from her hands and hanging them back up while Beau stood there trying to figure out what in the hell he'd missed. Mary and Drake? Who was this Alyssa, if not Drake's girlfriend?

"He was showing them to me," she said simply.

Chase laughed out loud. "Like you've never seen them before. I'm guessing you started using them before you were out of grade school."

"Yeah, I think I was in third grade when my father finally started letting me groom my own horse without assistance. Of course, I was probably five when I started trying. If I was old enough to ride, I was old enough to groom, but he always rechecked everything to make sure I'd done a good job," she said.

Beau frowned. Third grade? Her own horse? Five?

"Was he giving you a test or something? What a kidder you are, Beau." Chase slapped his brother on the back.

Beau was still confused. Who in the hell is this girl?

Chase continued, "Why did you bring her into the barn when she's got her interview and meeting new people

5

clothes on? She's going to get them dirty, dumbass. Where's your luggage, Alyssa?"

"In the car."

"Great, let's go get it and I'll show you to your room. It's going to be great having you here for the next few months." Chase and Alyssa walked out into the sunshine.

Beau's brain finally caught up, after forcing its way through the haze of lust and anger. Alyssa Jefferson was the intern from CSU that was going to be working with them over the spring calving season. Her father was part of the Cattlemen's Association and had known his father for years. She was a barrel racer and a trick rider and had won awards for her riding. He groaned.

Alyssa was gorgeous and single and she was going to be working with him for months and he had just acted like the biggest asshat on the planet.

He threw his hat into the dirt. *Damn it all to hell. That's what I deserve for jumping to conclusions and letting my temper get the best of me.* How many times did he have to go around this same fricken mountain before he learned?

CHAPTER 2

*A*lyssa was so flippin' glad to get away from Beau. She had no idea how she had pissed him off, but she'd never, in her whole life, been treated so badly. Even the bullies at school had been less mean. If Chase hadn't come along when he did, she was certain she would have either thrown all the grooming tools at that man's head or burst into tears. Both reactions would have mortified her. She hoped she wouldn't have to work with him much—she knew one of the brothers was the family vet and was going to be working with her, and she prayed it was not Beau.

Chase was talking and she'd missed some of what he'd said. He was a well put together package himself, not as sexy as his brother, but a whole lot nicer. "...high altitude so make sure you stay hydrated. Don't walk out the door without a water bottle. I know you've got mountains back home, but you're starting from sea level there, unlike here where the mountains start a mile high and go up from there. The ranch sits at 8400 feet above sea level so when we go up in the hills it goes up from there. And sunscreen—don't forget sunscreen. We've got less atmosphere up here, so the sun is more intense and burns quicker. And it's dry up this high too, it's an alpine desert, so lotion and lip balm are now your best friends. We've got some new ones in the pantry if you need them. We set up a new supply every spring."

He stopped walking, glanced at her, then looked down at his boots. "Sorry, didn't mean to give you a lecture, but pretty girls like you make me nervous and I start spouting facts. Next time just punch me and tell me to shut the hell up."

Alyssa laughed and punched his shoulder. "It's okay, I appreciate the heads up, but I've been living in your alpine desert for three and a half years at school, so I've got plenty of sunscreen, lip balm, and lotion. Plus, a whole collection of water bottles. Obviously, this is a higher elevation than Fort Collins, so I'll be extra cautious. Thanks." She smiled at him and he smiled back, just as Beau walked out of the barn.

Beau stomped over to them. "Chase, are you going to stand around all day jawin' or are you going to get her luggage in the house? Alyssa, I um, well, I was kind of…."

Chase elbowed her as Beau stumbled over his words. Beau frowned at his brother and then turned that frown on her and barked out, "You're here to work, not flirt." Then he reached into her trunk and hefted her largest suitcase in one hand and her box of textbooks in the other and stomped off toward the house. She was mortified by his words, and awed by his strength.

Chase stood there watching him walk away, then he turned to her and said, "What in the hell is wrong with him? He's got a burr under his saddle about you."

Alyssa shook her head. "I have no idea, he's been acting like that since I got out of the car."

"Just so you know, you're welcome to flirt with me anytime you want." Chase winked at her to let her know he was teasing. "Let's get the rest of your stuff in before Mr.

Grumpy comes back out. We'll get your riding gear into the barn after you meet everyone else."

"Sounds good." Chase took her other suitcase and hooked her backpack over his shoulder leaving her to carry in her hat boxes and purse.

"Don't I feel like the princess with just my hat boxes." She winced as she remembered Beau calling her princess, but didn't have time to dwell on it, because out of the house shot another man that looked so much like Chase that she had to do a double take. The only difference she could see was that Chase had on a blue shirt and the new guy had on a green one.

Chase laughed. "My twin, Cade."

Cade's eyes sparkled with mischief. "Nice to meet you, Alyssa. Here, let me take those." He reached out and took her hat boxes. "I'm the good-looking brother—you sure are a pretty little thing." He smiled at her. "Welcome to the Rockin' K. We are going to have an awesome time." He extended his arm for her to take, so he could escort her to the door that was less than twenty feet away.

She laughed at his silliness and put her hand in his arm and pinched. Cade laughed out loud, just as Beau appeared again. He glared at them and stomped off to the barn.

Cade looked at Chase and lifted an eyebrow.

Chase shrugged and started walking.

Cade whistled and muttered something that sounded like "Interesting" under his breath.

Alyssa looked toward the barn where Beau had disappeared and wondered again what was wrong with the man. He was sure sexy, but he had such a nasty personality she didn't want to be within fifty feet of him. But hanging out with the cute twins wouldn't be a hardship.

～

BEAU STOMPED INTO THE BARN. He had to get a grip on himself, he was still acting like a raging asshole but couldn't seem to stop. Every time Alyssa smiled at one of his brothers he saw red. And her hand tucked into Cade's arm had made him want to tear his brother's head off. What in the holy hell was wrong with him? He had never felt this kind of fury in his entire life. What was it about Alyssa that made him into a monster? It was crazy and he had no control over it.

He'd gone out to see if he could apologize for acting like a dick when she'd first arrived, and she had been standing by her car smiling at his brother. Her eyes sparkled and her grin covered her whole face. Chase had been beaming back at her with a sappy half in love expression on his face and Beau had wanted to punch him right in the nose. He'd lectured himself the whole time he was carrying in her suitcase and books. But the minute he stepped out the door a second time to apologize, she'd been hanging on Cade. Enough. He was going to avoid her like the plague.

Mary's riding lesson would keep him occupied for the next hour; she and Drake should arrive soon, so he should probably saddle up a couple of horses. The two of them could ride in the corral to get her comfortable on the animal.

He busied himself getting the horses ready. He'd already picked a gentle mare for Mary, so he selected a nice calm gelding for Drake. Drake could handle about any kind of horse, but this gelding would help the mare stay calm. Normally he wouldn't start out with just putting a new person on a horse, but he was too rattled to start with the basics and getting to know the horses first. Beau was agitated enough, he would probably get the horses riled up and that wasn't a good idea.

Drake and his new girlfriend, Mary, arrived. Beau walked over to the black SUV Drake drove as the town sheriff. Drake was opening the door for his girlfriend. As she stood up, Beau groaned at his stupidity but managed a smile for the two of them. "Drake, good to see you."

His friend nodded and smiled at his forty-something girl-friend. "Beau, this is Mary. Mary, this is Beau. He's going to give you some riding lessons."

Beau shook hands with Mary and decided he was a lunatic to think Drake would have hit on Alyssa. Mary was a pleasant woman the same age as Drake—maybe a few years younger but still in the ballpark. Inwardly chastising himself for being a fool, he wondered how he was going to ever apologize to Alyssa for being such a dumbass. Telling her he had thought she was the play thing of a man old enough to be her father wasn't an option. She would be insulted and probably deck him. He had to think of some way to convince her he wasn't completely insane.

The whole time he was giving the lesson he wondered about what Alyssa and his brothers were doing. He had to get a grip on himself, this fascination was ridiculous. She'd been on the ranch an hour and he'd gone bat-shit crazy.

CHAPTER 3

*A*lyssa's head was spinning by the time she'd been introduced to the whole family. Four generations of Kiplings lived in the house. Grandpa K, as he preferred to be called, was pushing eighty. He looked rascally with a twinkle in his eye and a quick mind. Cade had introduced her to the man, who was standing in the kitchen clearly waiting for her.

"Grandpa K, this is Alyssa Jefferson." Cade turned to her. "Alyssa, my grandfather Rupert Kipling."

Alyssa reached out her hand. "Nice to meet you, sir."

"There will be none of that siring or mister. I am Grandpa K and I expect you to call me that—same as everyone else does, little lady." He shook her hand, and his blue eyes twinkled with mirth.

She grinned. "I can do that, Grandpa K."

"I knew your grandfather a little. We met a time or two at the Cattlemen's Association. Seemed like a good guy. You were probably too little to remember him before he passed on."

She nodded as her throat tightened a bit. She had a vague memory of a man who smelled like peppermint, but that was about all. Her oldest brother had confirmed it was her dad's father who always had peppermints on him.

"A good man. Well, welcome to the Rockin' K. I hope you have a fun time and learn a lot, Alyssa." Turning to the twins he said, "Your mom and dad are in the office with Adam."

Alyssa cleared her throat and managed to say goodbye to Grandpa K.

As they walked out she glanced around the friendly farm kitchen as she followed the twins. Painted in shades of blue with blue speckled enamelware accents, it had a large table and plenty of counter space for preparing meals. There was an old yellow dog in a bed that's tail thumped once in what she supposed was a greeting.

Alyssa trailed the twins past the living room down the hall to an office. Chase knocked once on the door and then opened it and they all three trooped in, the twins still carrying her luggage. The office was large and had three desks in it, and a conversation area in the fourth corner. One wall was nearly all book shelves brimming with books on ranching and stacks of magazines. She could see from the door that some of the books were similar to the older birthing record journals they had at her home. Many of the books and magazines were familiar as well. But there were some she'd never seen. She would have to ask if she could read them while she was here. The three adults in the room looked up from their discussion. A young man, who she assumed was Adam, was sitting on a corner of one desk while his mother sat in the desk chair and his father stood behind her. They all had the same good looks she'd seen in the family members she'd already met.

Cade was, again, the spokesman. "Mom, Dad, Adam, this is Alyssa Jefferson, here for her internship. Alyssa, this is my mom and dad, Travis and Meg Kipling and my oldest brother, Adam."

Travis and Meg came around to the front of the desk and Adam joined them. Alyssa smiled and shook hands with each one. "Mr. and Mrs. Kipling, thank you so much for inviting me into your home. Nice to meet you, Adam."

Meg Kipling was a pretty woman with warm brown eyes and almost black hair pulled up in a twist, she wore jeans and a flannel shirt. She laughed. "Welcome to our home, Alyssa. Please call me Meg." She frowned at her sons. "Boys why are you dragging Alyssa's belongings all over the house? Go on and take her things to her room. We'll take good care of her."

The twins looked sheepishly at each other. "Yes, ma'am," they said in unison and headed out the door.

Travis Kipling's eyes sparkled, just like his father's had, when he said, "Now Meg, what did you expect those two to do when presented with a pretty little thing like Alyssa here?" He turned to Alyssa with a wide grin. "Welcome to the Rockin' K, Alyssa. If the boys get to be too much, let me know, and I'll give them something to keep them busy."

Alyssa blushed and started to stammer out something incoherent, but Adam interrupted, bless him.

"Alyssa, welcome to the crazy farm. You'll get used to us." He shook his head at his parents. "Or not. So, who haven't you met yet? You've met the twins and Grandpa and the three of us."

Alyssa nodded. "And Beau."

"Drew's on patrol right now—he's the rebel in the family, leaving the ranching life to become one of the town cops. He'll be here after his shift, for dinner. That just leaves Emma and Tony."

Just as Adam finished speaking, a pretty woman about Alyssa's age walked in holding the hand of a little boy who looked to be about four.

Adam grinned. "And here they are, right on time. Em, Tony, this is Alyssa Jefferson. She's our veterinary intern this semester. Alyssa, this is my sister Emma and her son Tony, short for Anthony."

Emma reached out to shake Alyssa's hand, letting go of Tony. "Hi, Alyssa. We are going to have great fun with you here. Tony, say hello to Alyssa." She looked down to her side, but Tony wasn't there any longer—he was hiding behind his mother and peeking out at Alyssa. "Oh, sorry. I guess he's feeling shy today. You never know about them at this age. Shy one minute, climbing all over you the next."

Alyssa laughed and winked at Tony. "Think nothing of it—my dad and step-mom had twin boys when I was twelve. One is outgoing the other is more reticent. He'll come around, eventually, and we'll be best friends."

"That's very likely. Have you been to your room yet? Let me show you where it is."

Meg nodded. "Good idea, Emma. Alyssa, dinner is at six thirty, please join us then, and you're welcome in any of the other rooms at any time—but feel free to unpack and settle in."

Emma turned to her son. "Tony, do you want to come with me and Alyssa, or stay with Nana and Papa?"

He peeked out from behind his mother and looked at Alyssa with his big brown eyes. She smiled at him. He looked at his grandparents and back at Alyssa, clearly torn. "Mama and Lyssa."

"Come along, then." Emma held out her hand to her son, who shook his head and sidled up to Alyssa holding out his tiny hand to her.

She felt a grin spread across her face as she took the little, somewhat sticky, hand in hers.

Emma shook her head. "See? No shyness left, but I see some major flirting going on. Already a lady killer, just like his uncles."

"From what I've seen so far, he's got some good role

models in that area." *Except for one notable exception, that is.*

~

BEAU FINISHED THE RIDING LESSON. Mary had done a good job. She was a little timid at first but as they walked the horses around and around in the corral, she'd become more at ease. And she had enjoyed brushing her mare down afterward. He would take them for a ride in the pasture when she came back next week, weather permitting. Springtime in the mountains of Colorado was always a crap shoot. It could be seventy degrees and sunny one minute and snowing like crazy the next. Bad weather could move into the area in a heartbeat. In the summer, it was lightning storms instead of snow, but still unpredictable.

It was nearly dinner time, but Beau was stalling on going into the house. He should at the least wash up, but he wasn't ready to face Alyssa yet. He'd been such an ass to her. Could he pretend nothing had happened and ignore the previous encounters? One thing for certain he couldn't stay in the barn all night. Someone would come looking for him if he didn't get his butt in the house. Even Drew was home from his shift as a town cop. All the chores were done—he had no more excuses, so he turned the lights off and headed in to face the music.

He hung his coat in the mud room and kicked off his boots before he scrubbed up in the big sink and ran his wet fingers through his hair to get it to behave. Time had run out for him to change out of his work clothes since he'd spent too much time in the barn. His mother didn't like anyone to be late for dinner unless they had a damn good excuse—and he didn't—so his work clothes were going to have to do, fortunately it had been an easy day, so he wasn't filthy.

The kitchen was empty and the table wasn't set. His

mother must be trying to impress Alyssa by eating in the dining room. Which meant everyone else would have changed into clean clothes except him. Well hell, this day was just getting better and better.

He walked into the dining room where everyone was already seated and slid into his chair. "Sorry I'm late. I was finishing up...." He let his sentence trail off because frankly, he hadn't been finishing a damn thing.

His father raised an eyebrow, knowing nothing was urgent, but didn't say anything.

His mother said, "You're right on time. You can give the blessing."

He groaned inwardly while smiling outwardly. That was his mother's way of saying he'd blown it. "Happy to. Heavenly Father, thank you for this meal we are about to eat. Bless the hands that prepared it, and may it nourish our bodies. Thank you for bringing Alyssa safely to the ranch and we ask for your blessing on her internship with us." *And dear God, please help me not to be an asshole.* "In Jesus' name, we pray. Amen."

When he looked up Alyssa gave him a weak smile, and he returned it. Better than her throwing mashed potatoes at his head—or a knife. Thankfully, chaos reigned at the dinner table and Alyssa seemed to be perfectly at ease with it. Little Tony sat between Alyssa and Emma; he seemed quite taken with Alyssa. All men, from four on up, appeared to be attracted to the woman. The food was passed around the table and everyone filled their plates.

After a few bites, Beau's father cleared his throat. "Alyssa, you mentioned earlier that your father and step mother had twins when you were twelve. How many kids are in your family?"

"There are six of us all together. I have two older brothers, and the three little ones are from my father's second marriage. I have a sister that's twelve now and my younger brothers are ten. My mom passed away when I was six. Dad remarried, after some prodding by his know-it-all daughter, when I was eight."

His dad burst out laughing. "It sounds like there is a story behind that statement."

"Oh, yes, I was quite the pistol at the wise old age of eight. I decided it was time for my dad to remarry and I decided my third-grade teacher was the perfect choice. Let's just say I put on quite the campaign to get them together. My best friend, Rachel, helped me devise Operation Naughty. O.N. was to get my father into the school on a regular basis, so they could fall in looove." Alyssa laughed, and Beau felt the sound shimmer through him like liquid sunshine.

She shook her head. "Thank goodness they were attracted to each other. It all worked out in the end, but that was just pure luck on my part. Of course, I still tease them about me being the best matchmaker ever. And all of us mock them both about wearing their best clothes the first time they went on a date, which was a trail ride. My teacher showed up in a silk blouse and my father had on his best boots. Being a precocious and completely clueless eight-year-old, I told my teacher she shouldn't be riding horses in her pretty blouse and then asked my dad why he had on his good boots. They were both embarrassed and changed before we rode out."

While everyone laughed at the story, Alyssa looked straight at him and raised an eyebrow. He nodded at her clear set down. He'd been put in his place and only the two of them knew it. She was good. Clearly the score was Alyssa one, Beau zero—or maybe minus ten. Who was winning? Not him, that was for damn sure. She had a few more things she could call him out over, and he was certain she would get to it eventually. And he might just enjoy every minute of it when she did.

CHAPTER 4

*A*lyssa pulled on a sweater over a flannel shirt and T. The key to living in Colorado was to dress in layers. Several garments would keep her warm if it was cold, and if it heated up she could remove an item or two. It could be thirty degrees in the morning and seventy in the afternoon.

She ran a brush through her hair and pulled it up into a pony tail while surveying her room. It was pleasant with a queen-sized bed she had been comfortable sleeping in. On top of the blankets and sheets there was a lovely quilt that looked like it was hand made. It sported a starburst design with red, orange and yellow, some of her favorite colors, so it made her happy to look at it. She wondered if someone in the family had sewn it, or whether it had been bought at some town festival. Back home they had a lady that made beautiful quilts and had put them in the art gallery when it opened a few years ago.

The room had a large chest of drawers, a tiny desk just big enough for her laptop, and even a fireplace. She imagined it would be handy to have a fire to keep warm if the electricity went out during a winter storm. She had a large closet that handily stored all her clothes and suitcases. There was a shared bathroom across the hall, but she didn't know who she was sharing it with for sure—she guessed maybe Tony and Emma, because there didn't seem to be any manly products in there. The window in her room looked over the driveway toward the main road. She wished it had a view of the mountains, but she would need to spend her free time resting—not daydreaming over the snowy peaks. She was there to work and learn, and if they started early in the day, like they did back home, she wanted to get going.

She carried her work boots with her. She would put them on when she was ready to head outside. Until then they would be in the mudroom with everyone else's footwear. She padded through the house in her stockinged feet and set her boots by the door. She could smell coffee brewing even though it wasn't yet light outside. Cattlemen started the day early, and that meant plenty of coffee to get the blood moving.

She was a little nervous to see Beau that morning. He'd been gracious when she'd set him straight at dinner last night, but she didn't know his character, so he could be just biding his time to snap at her again. She turned out of the mudroom and ran smack dab into six feet of hard muscle. Of course, it couldn't be any of the other six men in the house—it had to be Beau.

"Alyssa, good. I was hoping you were up. I need a hand."

There was an urgency in his tone and expression that caused the snarky comment on the tip of her tongue to evaporate. "What's up?'

"One of the cattle sounds distressed. I heard it from my room a few minutes ago. Can't see anything because it's too dark. We've had some trouble recently with wild cats—don't know if that's the problem, but it wouldn't surprise me.

Adam and Dad will be following me in a few minutes, but you're up and dressed, and they aren't."

"Let's go." She started pulling on her boots while Beau did the same. They yanked on jackets. Beau handed her a flashlight, and he grabbed a first aid kit and a rifle. She switched on the light and they headed out the door to investigate. Once outside, she could hear the ruckus he'd heard from his room. Something was not happy. She shone her flashlight around, but didn't see anything, so they followed the distressed sounds. She didn't know where they were headed and decided it was silly of her to have the flashlight.

"Beau, trade me the first aid kit for the flashlight. You know where you're going, and I don't."

"It's heavy."

She rolled her eyes, even though he couldn't see it. "Don't be ridiculous. I can manage it—we need to move quicker."

"True." He handed her the first aid kit and took the flashlight and was moving fast toward the sound.

Alyssa lugged the first aid kit. It was heavy, but the adrenaline from her concern for the animal carried her along in the man's wake. They headed in the opposite direction from the barn and corral—across some land that looked like it might be a summer garden—and past a building that probably housed the tractor and haying equipment. The bellowing was getting louder so they were close.

Beau hopped over the four-foot fence in front of them like it was nothing. Alyssa pushed the first aid kit under the split rail and clambered over it. Not pretty or gracefully, but she was quick. Beau was a few yards away bending over the injured animal. Alyssa moved up next to him. The cow was bleeding and its leg caught in a trap of some kind.

Alyssa hunkered down next to the heifer. "Poor thing. She calmed right down when you showed up."

"Yeah. Here, hold the flashlight on the trap so I can get it off her." He set the rifle on the ground and pried the metal off the heifer's back leg, which caused the bleeding to worsen. Beau held the wound closed while Alyssa flipped open the first aid kit. She pulled out gauze, to help staunch the blood flow, and the disinfectant. She was surprised that the cow hadn't fought Beau.

"Hand me the antiseptic."

She gave it to him. "That's going to sting. Do you want me to hold her?"

"Nope, no need. Just keep the light on the wound, so I can see." He poured the cleanser on the laceration, and other than a low moan and a small twitch there was no reaction.

Amazed, Alyssa watched the injured animal remain perfectly still while Beau stitched up and bandaged her leg.

Alyssa startled when Adam spoke from behind her. She hadn't sensed the two men approach.

"It's Dolly, isn't it."

Beau answered, "Yep."

Adam said, "That looks like a beaver trap."

"Yep."

"Dad and I brought transport, so we can get her to the barn and keep an eye on her for a few days. It's by the gate—I'll go get it."

Travis took the flashlight from her hand. "Alyssa, go with Adam. You can help with the gate."

Alyssa stood and noticed the sun was almost up, illuminating the uneven ground. She followed Adam and when they were twenty yards away from Beau she asked him about the animal.

"I've never seen an animal lie perfectly still like Dolly did. Is Beau some kind of heifer whisperer?"

Adam laughed. "No. When Dolly was a calf a big cat went after her and clawed her up pretty bad. Before her mother took on the cat. We heard the commotion and rode in to see what was happening. Dad got out the rifle and shot the cat, but Dolly's mother didn't make it. We took the calf back to the barn and had a vet come in to look at her. He suggested putting her down, but Beau pestered him enough that he dressed the wounds, but still told Beau he didn't think she would make it without her mother. Beau made the vet tell him everything he needed to do to save the calf, and then he followed those instructions to the letter. Beau saved her life. She's past child-bearing age, but there is no way we are doing anything but letting that cow live out her natural life in luxury."

Alyssa marveled at the story. "But he had to be just a child at that time."

"Yeah, he was about ten, I think. You've never seen a kid so committed to a task as Beau was to Dolly. That's how she got her name—we teased him about his giant dolly. It never fazed him, he was dedicated to saving her life. Beau became a vet in order to have the knowledge to save other animals like Dolly."

Alyssa groaned inwardly. She was going to be spending every day with the man. He was clearly a talented veterinarian, but she would have picked any of the other brothers, over him, to work with twelve hours a day.

They got to the transport vehicle which was already through the gate. She laughed. "So why did your dad want me to come with you? You don't really need help with the gate."

"Nah, we left this here so we didn't startle the animal with it. If we'd known it was Dolly, we could have driven it right up to her. But Beau was pissed." Adam ticked off on his fingers the strikes against the perpetrators. "The trappers are using an illegal device, they didn't ask permission to be on our land, and Dolly got caught in something that should have been submerged, not on dry land. Dad's going to talk Beau down, so he doesn't go off halfcocked looking for the people who hurt his cow. Beau's a good guy and normally pretty laid back, but he's got a short fuse where his animals are concerned—especially Dolly."

Alyssa had not seen Beau being laid back, so she had to wonder at Adam's definition of the phrase. She got into the transport vehicle and they headed back to Dolly. It didn't take long to get the animal loaded and headed back to the barn. Beau was silent the whole way as he sat in the back with Dolly. Alyssa didn't know what to say or do, so she just rode along in silence. When they got to the barn, the rest of the family was waiting to hear what had happened.

As they all gathered around Beau and Dolly, Alyssa slipped off to go get some coffee. She was glad the cow would be fine, but this seemed like a family moment and she wanted to give them time and space.

BEAU GOT DOLLY SETTLED in an empty stall. He gave her a little something for pain and made sure she had food and water readily available. He was still pissed at the cause of her injury, but decided to let the law handle it, as his father had suggested. His brother, Drew, would get an earful as soon as possible. They probably wouldn't be able to find the poachers, but Beau would make sure they had every bit of information he knew, just in case.

He was damn glad Alyssa had been up and dressed when he hit the back door. She'd been a trooper—he would have needed to wait for his father or brother if she hadn't been ready, and that would have been dangerous for Dolly. He didn't know when Alyssa had left the group—probably when his family had descended like a horde of locusts. But he wanted to find her and thank her for her help. That was quite the initiation for her first few hours on the ranch. But she'd handled it just fine. She hadn't questioned him or complained about carrying the thirty-pound first aid kit. She'd kept up with him and hadn't driven him crazy with a million questions. But she'd been prepared to help hold down the hurt animal if he'd needed her to. He was quite impressed with her. She was a whole lot more than just a pretty face.

Alyssa sat at the kitchen table, shoveling in breakfast. His mother dished him up a plate while he washed his hands. After setting his food and a large mug of coffee on the table, his mother left the two of them alone in the kitchen. He was glad, since he had some things he needed to say to Alyssa.

After a large gulp of coffee, he said, "Thanks for going with me this morning. You were a big help."

"I'm here to work," she said sweetly.

He groaned. "I'm really sorry for my attitude yesterday. It was uncalled for. I said a lot of things I would like to cut my tongue out for saying. Can you forgive me?"

"I can, and will, but I reserve the right to throw it in your face from time to time." She grinned up at him. "You good with that, cowboy?"

"I can be." He held out his hand. "Pacts?"

She shook it. "Pacts."

Beau didn't want to let go of her hand. It was soft and warm and just that small touch sent a flood of warmth through him, pushing the anger and frustration of the last few hours away. He pulled back reluctantly, and Alyssa looked down at her breakfast like she was doing surgery. He didn't know what to think either, so he followed suit. What in the hell was *that* about? He'd never felt anything like it from simply shaking hands with a woman. *Okay then, no more touching the girl.*

CHAPTER 5

*A*lyssa and Beau settled into an uneasy peace. Spring calving season was coming up quickly, and Beau needed to get her familiar with where everything was. And how they handled the season in Colorado, where it was a lot colder, and they had to be aware and ready for any weather difficulties.

Beau asked Alyssa, "So, you have cold weather in your hometown, correct?" He didn't know a lot about where she was from—just the eastern part of Washington. Why he was so curious about her home he had no idea, so he decided to chalk it up to knowing the differences in their experience. That was a convenient excuse for his nosiness.

"Yes, but not much snow, or even a lot of rain. We're next to the mountains and they get snow on them up higher, but down near the lake it's more temperate. Once every five years, or so, we get dumped on for Christmas, but it's not the norm."

He nodded. "So, it's a large lake?"

"Yes, in comparison to the lakes in this area, our lake is about five times the size of Lake Granby."

He whistled. "No wonder it keeps things more temperate. That's a lot of water. Plus, our elevation here is probably starting where yours taps out in the mountains. So, we're dealing with a lot more cold, and a lot more snow."

"Yeah, we've got some fourteeners in the Cascades, but the peaks along the lake run up to about eight thousand feet, which is the elevation here, isn't it? Will we have weather difficulties during the birthing season?"

"Very possibly. It can snow here right up until June. Not every day of course, but during harsh winters it can be a challenge. Winter wasn't bad this year, so maybe we'll get lucky."

While Beau familiarized Alyssa with the ranch routine and taught her the procedures used for birthing at the Rockin' K, the rest of the crew would spend the next week bringing the younger pregnant dams in closer to the house—so everyone could keep an eye on them to be ready to help with any trouble the mothers would have delivering. The older the heifer was the easier they gave birth. Some could still have trouble, so they would be checking on the whole herd which were already in the nearest pasture, but they brought the two-year-old mothers in closest, with the older cows who'd had breech births or other difficulties previously, next in line. Once a dam produced a breech calf the likelihood of her subsequent babies being breech was increased. And other delivery problems seemed to follow the same pattern.

Birth weight was another concern—the longer it took for the mother to deliver, the more difficult it could be. Purely due to the calf's size.

Beau went over where everything was located, how they would handle the rotation and birthing stalls, what he wanted her to concentrate on, and how they would communicate. They exchanged cell phone numbers and Beau gave her a list of all the ranch hands to program into her phone, and suggested she make a group text with all the family in it, and send out her number as the first group text.

"So now that you've had the grand tour and know where everything is, do you have any questions?"

Alyssa shook her head. "Not right now, but I'm sure I will after we get started. Now that my head isn't spinning from everything you've shown me the last couple of days, do you have any copies of the birthing records I could start looking at? I think it would be helpful to have some ideas of what to expect. I used to help my dad with keeping the records for our small herd. We have everything in a database online, with paper backup copies. I would guess—with your herd the size it is—you've gone digital also."

"Yeah, we have. And I can tell you that I am happy we don't have to do it all on paper like the old journals in the house. We do keep paper copies just in case, but the software saves everything to the cloud and is supposed to be fool proof. Being paranoid, we also have a backup that runs each night to an external drive here on the ranch. It took Adam and I a few years to get my dad and grandpa to trust the database to be our primary source of record keeping."

She laughed. "Losing the records would be awful so I understand. I've looked through some of those old records at home. What a mess they are. I'm happy to be digital too.

"I have a Surface you can use while you're here, it's half tablet, half computer it's made by Microsoft… and you live in Washington, so you probably know all about them."

"Maybe just a little." She teased.

He chuckled. "Anyway, it's already set up with access to the software and database all you need is the password. We've got several portable machines like the Surface, so we can take them out in the pasture for reference. This one is for your use, as my helper, we'll be the ones in charge of the database. The hired hands write up everything on paper, I don't quite trust them to have access to the database. The rest of the family has the passwords so they can look things up, but they leave me—and now you—to do updates. Anyway, I'm sure we keep the same types of records, but I might have to teach you my shorthand."

She laughed. "I imagine each ranch has their own way of keeping track of all that information. Written out long hand it would take a ton of books. Isn't it great to have technology?"

Drawn into her enthusiasm for the work, and her sparkling eyes and throaty laughter that sent shivers through him, Beau vowed to ignore the attraction. Again. "We have the field notes and backup paper copies of course just in case we lose power or whatever, but yes the technology makes things a lot faster and easier."

He gave Alyssa the small computer and the passwords and showed her the software they used.

She grinned. "We use the same software, so you won't have to teach me how to use it."

"Perfect, so it's just my short hand you'll need to learn. I do a lot in code, so I don't have to write it out for three hundred new calves."

They went over a couple of the calving records, so he could explain his notes. But sitting that close to her—pouring over information—on a ten-inch screen was making him crazy. Her scent was intoxicating, and he needed to move out of the danger zone immediately—if not sooner.

He stood up before she could ask any more questions. "I've got a couple of things to do. Go ahead and start looking over the information and if you can't interpret something make a list and I can go over it with you later. You can stay out here in the office or take the tablet into the house—it's on Wi-Fi and we have it boosted, so we can access the data nearly anywhere on the property. Some of the far out grazing land has some holes in coverage, but even then, we can switch over to satellite—if we need to. It costs a fortune, so we don't do it often, but it's an option."

Once he was out of her vicinity he relaxed. She could study up on the most likely cases of calving difficulties while he tried to cool down. She asked good questions and wanted to study their herd, so she would understand where the challenges could lie. That proved to him she was serious about the job, he couldn't be happier with her as an intern. But he could only handle a short amount of time in close proximity, before his body started reacting to her. He'd never felt such a pull from a woman before, but he was going to fight it with everything he had. She was too young for the likes of him and lived halfway across the continent too. Okay maybe that was an exaggeration, but it took a couple of days to drive there, anyway.

ALYSSA WAS a little shocked when Beau got up and left. She was learning a lot from him. He was an intelligent man and patient with her and all her questions. She'd had to fight not to lean into him when they were looking at the data on the Surface; he was so warm and smelled good, too. She hadn't quite acclimatized to the cold at this elevation—even though she was dressing in layers—her hands were always cold. So, Beau being all warm and toasty made her want to snuggle. Not exactly a professional attitude for her to be having, so she had been valiantly ignoring the idea, and was enjoying his explanation of the notes he took on each animal. He was amusing when he wasn't being a jerk. She still hadn't decided what had happened that first day, but he'd been pleasant since the incident with Dolly. Fortunately, Dolly was healing well.

Alyssa shrugged at Beau's abrupt departure and got a little notepad to write down questions she had for him as she looked through the database on the cattle.

A couple hours later, she was still poring over the database and noticed some trends she wanted to ask Beau about when she saw him next.

Cade burst through the door. "What are you doing out here Alyssa? It's nearly dinner time."

Alyssa startled at his abrupt entrance. "Is it really? I had no idea." She noticed that the Surface was running low on power, so she would have to plug it in to recharge. "I'll shut down the database and come with you. Beau said I could bring the surface with me."

Cade laughed. "My God, you're as bad as Beau. He's been known to spend hours poring over birthing records, and you've been doing the same, haven't you."

"Guilty as charged," she said as she stood with a groan. "I've clearly been sitting too long, hunched over this machine." She stretched her back and shoulders, reaching up to the ceiling and then down to the floor. Then, she picked up the computer, charger, and her notepad and looked over at Cade, who seemed frozen.

Alyssa asked, "What's wrong? Let's get moving."

"Um yeah, just well, that was freaking hot."

"What was hot? My stretching? That's ridiculous, let's go." She pushed past him.

"It's not ridiculous, Alyssa. You're a beautiful, sexy woman." He followed her toward the house.

"Pssht, don't be silly. I'm just a female—like... like your sister." She pushed open the door into the mudroom and used the boot jack to help her get her boots off.

"But you're not my sister, so I can think you're hot if I want."

Beau came around the corner. "No, Cade, you can't. She's here as an intern not as something for you to lust after."

Alyssa guffawed and poked Beau in the chest. "Well, at least you're not accusing *me* this time." She pushed past Beau into the kitchen and went straight to her room to plug in the Surface. *Men are very odd beings.*

CHAPTER 6

*B*eau was seething. How dare his brother lust after Alyssa. Yes, she was beautiful and yes, she was sexy, but she didn't need some punk kid panting after her. And he didn't give a damn that he was being irrational. Cade was only two years younger than he was, and probably five years older than Alyssa, so he wasn't a punk kid. But it still chapped him to have his younger brother acting like a horn dog. Not that he had any real reason to talk since he was doing pretty much the same thing, but at least he knew he shouldn't be yearning for her. Cade wasn't fighting the attraction at all and had joked about it. Which had made Beau see red.

He knew he'd pissed Cade off too, by telling him to quit acting like a horn-dog and leave the woman alone. They'd nearly come to blows in the mud room before Chase had come in and drug his twin away. Beau didn't know why it had made him so angry; he'd joked with Cade in the past about sexy women, and who got dibs on them. But the idea of treating Alyssa with the same attitude made him a little crazy. And he really did not want to think about why that was. Maybe he should just dunk his head in the horse tank—the cold water might shock some sense into him.

He'd spent the whole afternoon working to stay away from her, only to come unhinged when his brother told her she was hot. He was glad Alyssa had laughed and brushed it off like it was no big deal. He needed to get his mind off the whole episode, before he had to sit at the same table with Alyssa and his brother.

He went into the kitchen to see if there was something that needed doing for dinner. Cooking relaxed him and gave him something else to think about. They had a rotation on who cooked each day—but he was never put on it anymore—at least not during calving season. He'd totally forgotten his turn one day almost two years ago. He'd been working on a difficult delivery and hadn't remembered to tag one of the other family members to ask them to take his slot. He'd not even remembered after the birth. He'd dragged himself in about an hour after dinner should have been, to find a jar of peanut butter and a loaf of bread with his name on it and the word *Dinner* written underneath. It had still taken him a moment to figure it out. Since then, the only time he was in charge of meal preparation was when they were haying or riding fence—and even then, his mom always checked in with him to make sure he was actually in the kitchen.

He found both his parents in the kitchen. His father was cutting up the roast while his mother made gravy.

"Can I help with something?"

His mother smiled at him. "Sure, would you like to make a salad? Everything else is about ready. Just have to finish the gravy and Tony wants to mash the potatoes."

"My pleasure." Beau went to the fridge and got all the vegetables he could find and set them on a large cutting board. He washed what needed washing and started in, dumping each new ingredient into the giant bowl. Minutes later he was in the zone, chopping and dicing, peeling and slicing. He barely noticed Tony and Emma come in to mash the potatoes. The salad bowl was filled to the brim with enough food for two families the size of his. Alyssa came up and snatched a cucumber slice out of the bowl.

She laughed. "Think you've got enough salad, cowboy? I think that would feed the entire state of Colorado."

He shrugged and set the knife down—so he didn't cut his fool thumb off while distracted by Alyssa. "Salad keeps for a day or two. It'll get eaten, don't you worry."

"Of that I have no doubt. You all eat like…" she bumped him with her hip, "…ranch hands."

Beau groaned. "You've been saving that one, haven't you?"

Alyssa grinned. "Not at all, but my family is sick and tired of hearing it. I have a brand-new audience here in Colorado."

Beau shook his head slowly. "We've brought a monster into our midst. And here the school said you were a great student and would be an asset."

"Did they now? Well, I am a good student, and I will be helpful—so they didn't lie. They just didn't let you in on my sense of humor. *Bwah ha ha.*" She rubbed her hands together, cackling gleefully.

"Alyssa?"

"What?"

"Get the salad dressing."

She laughed again, and Beau practically shivered as the sound shimmered through him. The woman was tying him in knots and she'd only been here a few days. He took off like a shot toward the table.

ALYSSA FOLLOWED Beau to the table. The man was so flippin' hot. When she'd walked in and saw him chopping up the salad she had practically drooled. The sight of a man in the kitchen, working away, was so appealing to her. She'd had a couple of boyfriends growing up who thought it was the woman's place to be in the kitchen and they wouldn't step foot into it. She'd dumped those immature idiots like a hot rock.

Her father was widowed when she was six and he hadn't whined about cooking; he'd taken on the job as nothing more than what had to be done. Her mom had been sick for a couple of years before she passed, and she'd carefully taught her husband how to make everything from simple meals to Thanksgiving dinner. Later, when her step-mother had come into the picture, her dad didn't stand aside and assume Ellen would make all the meals. He just kept on cooking right alongside his new wife. So, in reality, Alyssa had never seen anything different.

She was glad the others in the kitchen had been focused on little Tony attempting to mash potatoes. So, they didn't notice her stop dead in her tracks to watch Beau chopping the veggies. His strong hands and arms had mesmerized her for a minute until a piece of potato nearly smacked her in the forehead.

The flying spud had startled her out of her daze and got her moving again. She was certain the potatoes would be interesting to eat. She remembered her father letting her help cook at a young age and wondered if she'd made as big of a mess as Tony had—most probably. But she figured that's how children learned and if a person wasn't willing to clean up a little mess, then they probably shouldn't be having kids in the first place.

The potatoes were a disaster, very few of them were mashed, most were still in whole chunks.

Grandpa K was the first one to take a big bite of potatoes.

"Mmmm, these are delicious taters. I do declare they are some of the best I have ever eaten. Who made these?"

"I did Gampa K," Tony declared.

Grandpa K looked closely at Tony. "You made these fine spuds, Tony? Really? Are you big enough to make fine mashed potatoes like these?"

"Yes, I did. Nana helped cook 'em but I smashed 'em."

"You did a mighty fine job, young man. Mighty fine.

The little boy glowed with pride. Everyone took at least two helpings and raved about what a good job Tony had done mashing them, and how delicious they were.

Alyssa fell a little bit in love with the whole family.

She'd gleaned a bit of information that Emma was an unwed mother and that the father had been passing through town the spring of her senior year in high school, never to be seen again. But the family treated her with love, and there was no condemnation or shame about the situation.

Emma was a full-time mother and was getting a degree in accounting in online night school classes. She also did some bookkeeping for a few stores in town on Saturdays when the family all took turns watching Tony. When Tony started school, Emma planned to do more accounting for their small town, eventually hoping to open her own CPA firm to service the various businesses in the area.

Alyssa noticed that sometimes Emma looked a little sad when she watched her son playing. Alyssa wondered about that, but didn't feel it was her place to ask—and it never lasted long, just a moment or two.

They finished up with dinner and Alyssa helped with the cleanup. She didn't see where Beau had gone, so she decided to wait to talk to him about the birthing records later. She wanted to study them a little longer anyway before she asked him about what she had found. She excused herself to go back to her room.

CHAPTER 7

*A*lyssa was in the middle of a hot dream, costarring Beau. When she startled awake, the bedside clock showed three in the morning. Did someone knock on her door? Another knock sounded. She hopped out of bed, grabbed her robe and slipped it on as she walked barefoot to the door and opened it.

"Sorry to wake you," Beau said quietly. "One of the dams is giving birth and it's a little too early, so I could use a hand in case the little guy needs some help."

She snapped out of the haze of lust the dream had put her in. "Of course, let me get some clothes on and I'll meet you downstairs in two minutes."

"Thanks."

Alyssa quickly pulled on jeans and a shirt, dragged a hair brush through her hair and pulled it up into a messy bun, put some mints in her pocket and one in her mouth and rushed down the stairs. It was about two weeks early for the calves to start dropping, but nothing that was particularly dangerous—the little guys could survive at this stage, but sometimes they did need some TLC to get them through the preemie stage. She'd been around enough early births, to know the ropes, and assumed anyone in the household had also, so she was glad Beau had come to her for assistance. He was treating her like a bona fide intern. When she'd signed up for an internship, she'd wondered if the ranchers would take her seriously or treat her like a little girl playing doctor. She was happy to see they were treating her like a professional.

Beau was waiting for her in the mudroom. She put on her boots and coat and followed him to the barn, where Drew was waiting with the mother that was clearly in labor.

"I was just getting home from patrol and heard this one laboring, so I got her into the barn and called you. I can stick around for a while if you need help. I'm off for the next two days so I can wait a while to sleep. Hi Alyssa."

Beau answered, "You did great, brother. You're welcome to stay, but you might want to put on something over your uniform."

"Hi back at you, Drew. Another set of hands is always welcome," Alyssa said.

Beau was checking the mother to see what the scoop was, and if they could stop the labor and keep the calf in a little longer. "Water's broke so this one's coming now. Drew, after you get some coveralls on, can you grab a couple of warming blankets? Alyssa, she looks to be nearly fully dilated already, so I don't think this is going to take long."

"Which heifer is this?" she asked.

"It's 13-218."

"So, she's due in sixteen days, right?"

"Yes, you've already memorized their due dates?" Beau asked.

"I started with the ones due soonest. This is her second baby so it's not uncommon for them to come early. 13-218 even delivered her first one a few days early. She must dilate too soon."

"Yeah, we'll give her one more chance to breed and bring her in with the two-year olds, so she's less mobile and we can keep an eye on her. Okay, I see some hooves coming—glad the little ones not breech."

Drew brought over the warming blankets and Alyssa and Beau were ready to help if the mother or baby needed it. They both had a hand on the mother to be able to tell how the contractions were coming and if there seemed to be any distress. But they wanted to allow the calf to come as naturally as possible. Nature didn't always need man butting in to try to help.

Alyssa said, "She seems to be doing well."

"I agree. The calf is in perfect position, so the heifer shouldn't tear too much. Looks like it's going to be an easy delivery—let's just hope the calf is fine."

As the delivery progressed they all relaxed and let nature take its course.

Drew said, "Guess I panicked a little, everything seems fine."

Beau shook his head. "No, Drew, you did perfect. This little one is coming too early and we wouldn't want it born out in the pasture. It will probably need some supplements and monitoring—that it wouldn't have gotten tonight—if you hadn't brought the mother into the barn. But I don't think you need to stay up if you're tired. Alyssa and I got almost a full night's sleep, so if you need some shut eye you can head on in."

Drew shrugged. "I'll hang, to make sure the little guy is good. I've got some adrenaline still pumping."

Alyssa chuckled. "Yeah, we've all been there, for sure."

∾

Beau could relax now that everything seemed to be working out smoothly. He wasn't thrilled with the mother delivering so early, but he'd wait until after it was born to see if there was any real danger.

They talked shop while the calf was being born. Once the birth was complete Beau weighed the little guy—he was a little underweight but not too bad. He tagged the baby and gave him back to his mother. The calf started nursing and everyone breathed a sigh of relief. He was early, but he would make it.

Beau was glad he'd gotten a couple of the stalls ready. They would need to get everyone busy in the morning mucking out the rest of the birthing stalls and putting clean straw in them. They had about sixty two-year-old mothers; a third were due in the early spring, and a third were due mid spring, and the rest in late spring. So, they needed all thirty cattle stalls ready, because there were always a few of the older dams that needed to be in a stall and kept close at hand.

Beau wanted to get the first twenty of the two-year-olds in their stalls in the next few days. They needed to set up a rotation for riding the herd. They had ten townies they needed to get into the bunk house for the next couple of months. There were a few with families in town that would need to be on a day shift—the rest would rotate so there was always a couple of guys in the pasture checking on the older heifers and a couple in the barn. His father and Adam probably already had the rotation all planned out.

Drew yawned. "Now that I've seen the little guy is good, I'm going to go catch some *Zs*. See you guys later."

"Night, Drew. Thanks for catching this one. He probably would have been okay in the pasture, but you never know for sure. Better safe than sorry." Beau punched his brother in the arm.

"No assaulting a police officer."

"Can't see that you are one, in the coveralls."

Drew shrugged. "Guess I can leave them here for next time. I didn't even get them dirty."

"Something to be thankful for," Alyssa said. She turned and started cleaning up the birthing straw.

Beau nodded and turned to help right the stall so the pair of livestock would be comfortable. He put away the medical supplies, filled the feeder, and refreshed the water.

Alyssa finished laying down the clean straw and dusted her hands. "I think we're good for tonight." She leaned back against the stall door and looked at the mother and baby, who seemed content in their new surroundings.

Beau walked over and stood next to her. "Yep, everything is looking good. Thanks for being quick to join me out here tonight."

"Of course, it's my job and my passion. I hope you don't mind, but Adam told me how you decided to become a vet and about your work with Dolly. I have a similar story. I wonder if all veterinarians have a like tale."

Beau laughed. "That would be my guess. It's not the most pleasant job, and it certainly isn't for the glory. I guess some people might do it for other reasons, like easy hours and the high pay." He gave her a silly grin with those words.

Alyssa snorted. "Right, easy hours. Three in the morning. And so far, I haven't made a cent, have you?"

"I work on the family ranch, so my work goes to the good of the family. I have money when I need it, but living at home makes it easy."

"The house is plenty big enough for everyone." Alyssa smiled.

"Yeah, for now. If any of us ever marries and starts having families of our own, it might get crowded. But so far, we're good. There's plenty of land to build on, so no worries there."

"So, how come none of you are married?" Alyssa grimaced. "Never mind, that is none of my business."

Beau shrugged. "None of us have found the right one, yet."

"Do you believe there is only one?"

"Hell, I don't know. Maybe there is more than one. But, so far, none of us have found even one—let alone multiple people—we would want to spend a life with." He shook his head, and wondered if he *would* find someone he wanted to come home to every day. He was pushing thirty, with no one on the horizon. Although he had to admit he wouldn't mind a small kiss from the little cutie standing next to him. He looked over at her and wondered. No, he needed to keep their relationship on a professional level. No kissing on the intern.

She grinned at him. "Well, I suppose that's better than finding multiple ones at the same time and starting a harem."

Beau laughed out loud. "You've got a point there. Let's go in and see if we can scare up some coffee."

"Right behind you."

CHAPTER 8

*T*he next few days were a flurry of activity. They got the birthing stalls mucked out and fresh straw put in them. They brought the first set of two-year-old mothers into the barn, and started riding the herd to look for any issues. Everyone pitched in to be ready. The preemie was doing well, nursing from his mother and gaining weight.

Dolly's leg was healing nicely, and poor Drew had gotten an earful from his older brother about poachers. They'd all ridden out to look for any other traps and had found only one other, near the beaver dams next to the Colorado River. Drew promised to do what he could, and said he would also file a report with the fish and game warden in the area. No one thought they would catch the trappers participating in illegal activity, but at least it was reported.

Fortunately, the weather was cooperating so far. A few flurries of snow early in the morning before sunrise was about all they had. Not even enough precipitation to make mud; days were cool but sunny.

Alyssa continued to study the birthing records in the

evenings. One morning, Beau walked into the barn where she was checking on the two-year-old mothers.

"Alyssa, come with me. Let's check on the herd. I've saddled us a couple of horses."

She was a little surprised by that, but didn't argue. Generally, when the cattle were this close to giving birth they took a vehicle out so they could weigh and tag any babies that were being born.

"The twins are going out too, and we can call them if we need a truck."

Beau was poetry in motion as he fluidly mounted his horse and he looked mighty fine sitting on the animal. She tried not to drool. Alyssa was short legged, so she wasn't nearly as graceful as she mounted, she felt clumsy and awkward. Which she hadn't felt on a horse since she was little. When they started out Beau rode like he was part of the horse and again she thought she might drool watching the beauty of the horse and the cowboy.

Once they got to the cattle Beau started asking her questions. It didn't take Alyssa long to figure out what Beau was doing. He was quizzing her on what she'd learned from the birthing logs.

Beau pointed out a mother. "That's 09-123, what can we expect from her?"

He'd already asked her about a couple of other ones and now he was trying to see if she really knew her information. "No, it's not. That one over there could be 09-123, this one here is the wrong breed. For the real 09-123, which I think is that one over there based on her markings, we can expect an easy delivery, and this will probably be the last year that you breed her. She's starting to get up there in years. We're hoping for no birth defects since she's on the older side. It's always a possibility, but you bred her with a strong bull, so the calf should be fine."

Beau nodded.

"Now this one here that you tried to trick me with, she looks like she could be 11-210 or maybe 13-060, but I'm betting it's 11-210. If she is 11-210 we need to keep an eye on her because she nearly rejected her calf last year—you had to coax her to accept it, so we want to make sure she accepts her baby this year. If she rejects it, you might decide not to breed her any longer, even though she produces good stock. She's a little too unpredictable to keep on, if she's going to reject her offspring. We should keep an eye out for any mothers that lose their calf, in case we need to graft hers onto a surrogate mother."

Beau grinned at her. "Excellent, Alyssa. You've done much better learning the herd than I expected. We've got three hundred and change in mothers—that's a lot to memorize."

"Thanks. I'm not just a pretty face you know." Shit, did she just say that? How vain could she get? She felt her cheeks heat. "I mean, I've been working hard to learn them, not that I'm pretty… or.…"

Beau leaned over and patted her knee. "I know what you meant. But just for the record, you are quite pretty, and you've got brains to back it up."

Alyssa looked at Beau and saw admiration in his gaze and maybe a little lust, too. Oh, my. She was caught in his snare and couldn't look away. She wanted to lean over and take a taste of his lips, she felt herself start to tilt toward him. It was not a good idea, but she couldn't stop herself.

His phone chimed with an incoming text, which broke the spell. He looked at it and swore. "We're needed on the other side of the pasture. Don't-Touch-My-Baby is giving birth, and the twins need us to hold onto the dam while they weigh and tag the calf."

"Oh, I read all about her. She's not a fan of you cowboys

taking her baby from her for the five minutes it takes. You lead, I'll follow."

~

BEAU STARTED out at a fast clip—not too fast to startle the cattle, but quick enough to get them across the pasture to give the twins a hand. He was glad the guys had texted him when they did. He'd been about two seconds from leaning over and kissing Alyssa. He didn't think she would mind if what he saw in her eyes was any indication, but it was unprofessional of him and she was too young—or he was too old. They had nothing in common, well besides their chosen profession, and ethics, and upbringing, and…. Okay, so they had a lot in common; that still didn't fix the age difference. And he didn't need to be thinking about that now, he had a job to do.

As he rode through the herd, across the pasture, to where the twins were, he kept an eye on the cattle he passed, just to make sure assistance wasn't needed elsewhere. His dad and Grandpa K where keeping an eye on the birthing stalls, and would call if they needed him. Helping to keep Don't-Touch-My-Baby from freaking out while they weighed and tagged the calf was important, but not if there was another emergency. He didn't see anything as he rode through and he was certain Alyssa was watching carefully, also.

He saw the pickup the twins had driven out, and not too far away was Don't-Touch-My-Baby; they were right on time as the rest of the calf slid out of the mother. As they slid off the horses and tied them to the truck, Beau said, "Alyssa, go around to the front and hold her head. Chase is on the left and I'll take the right while Cade weighs and tags the little one. You know what to do and how not to get hurt, right?"

"Yep, no problem. We've got ProtectiveMama on our

ranch, who's just like Don't-Touch-My-Baby. I've done this every year since I was old enough to help."

The whole operation took less than ten minutes, but you would think it was days the way Don't-Touch-My-Baby acted. She was not happy to be detained, while some guy took her calf to be weighed and tagged. As soon as they got the newborn back at her side she was happy as could be, and started eating, while the baby nursed.

Chase sighed. "You would never know that was the same cow that was screaming bloody murder two minutes ago. Thanks for riding to the rescue, you two."

Beau was looking across the herd. "No problem. Dammit, I don't see River-PITA, have you checked for her?"

Cade swore. "No, we were so busy with Don't-Touch-My-Baby that PITA slipped my mind."

"Alyssa and I will go and bring her back, then we're going to head home to see how it's going in the stalls. Call if you need to. I'll send a couple of hands out to finish the side Alyssa and I were on. Let's go Alyssa, we've got a stubborn Pain-In-The-Ass to bring back from the river."

Alyssa rode next to Beau as they left the herd and headed into the trees, that bordered the Colorado River, on the edge of this pasture. They had plenty of water troughs in the pasture for the animals, so they didn't need to go near the water. The snow melt would have the Colorado running high this time of year, so he hoped River-PITA was staying far enough away to be safe. He didn't know if it was the fresh running water that drew her or the sweetness of the grass that grew along the banks. But if she wasn't with the herd she was at the river and he didn't want her giving birth down there. PITA might know enough to stay away from the water, but her baby wouldn't.

"I think maybe we'll bring River-PITA into a stall, so she doesn't give birth down by the river."

"Yeah, the calf wouldn't know enough to stay away from the river and I imagine the snow melt has it running pretty fast right now," Alyssa said.

"My thoughts exactly.

"Although, she's never given birth by the river before, has she? Maybe she's smart enough to know better and just goes down when she knows it's early."

"You're giving her a lot of credit."

Alyssa shrugged. "She might deserve it."

"But she might not, and I don't want to take the risk of losing the calf."

"I suppose not, but I can understand the draw, it's pleasant down here in the trees with the water running nearby. Maybe she likes the sound."

Beau laughed. "So, I should get her a sound machine?"

Alyssa grinned. "Maybe you should."

"Yeah, I'll just tell dad we need to order her a sound machine for the barn. When he checks me into the looney bin, you have to promise to come visit."

"Oh, I will, and I'll bring you cookies and puzzles to put together, oh and a sound machine for soothing river sounds."

Beau guffawed. "Good one."

Alyssa pointed. "There she is."

"Stay here with the horses, I don't want her spooked."

Beau handed Alyssa his reins and took his rope and walked over to the heifer. She just kept munching on grass as he slipped the rope around her neck. She followed him as he walked back to get on his horse and they set off at a slow pace back to the ranch.

Beau thought this might be a good time to ask Alyssa about her plans after she graduated. "You'll graduate at the end of this year, won't you?'

"Yes, and then I'll go back home for the summer. But I am planning to return in the fall to get my Masters in

Biomedical Sciences with a specialization in Reproductive Technology."

That's a one year, non-thesis track, isn't it?"

"Yes, it's been my plan all along. We had some trouble one year with getting the cows impregnated. We needed another bull because one got sick and we couldn't get a new one in time, so we had a slim year. After that, dad started doing more artificial insemination and it intrigued me. So, I want to specialize in it. I haven't yet decided if I want to continue on to get a PhD or Doctor of Veterinary Medicine."

"The specialization sounds like a good choice to me, you could pretty much write your own ticket with that. And of course, either the PhD or DVM are good to have. I did the five year DVM program." Beau turned to see how PITA was doing. So, Alyssa had at least one more year of schooling. Interesting, that meant she'd just be on the other side of the mountain, instead of several states away. But the other side of the mountains was still a couple of hours drive. Not that it mattered to him. Once her internship was over, he probably would never see her again.

CHAPTER 9

*B*eau was confident that Alyssa would be an asset once the cattle started giving birth. He felt like she was capable of overseeing the simple cases. She had a good handle on procedures and drew good conclusions from reading over the historical records. He would like to see her in a difficult situation to see how she reacted, but he just couldn't predict if that would happen. There would certainly be some challenging births—it was a matter of when and where they would occur. But more importantly, how many happened at the same time.

His dad and Grandpa K were good in a pinch, and Adam was too. Plus, his mother was no slouch—she'd waded right into difficulties more than once. None of them had any vet schooling—but they had experience—and that was often much more valuable than an education. He wasn't completely clear on how much Alyssa had been able to help on her home ranch. She'd made a couple comments about them patting her on the head and treating her like a child. He was pretty sure his sister would say the same thing about being the youngest, but he knew he could call on her to lend a hand. As long as

Tony was safe and taken care of, she wouldn't hesitate. So, Alyssa's family probably felt the same way. They had a much smaller herd, so maybe they just didn't need her that often.

The Rockin' K had some pretty solid hired hands too, so he was confident it would be a good season. Busy yes, but not overwhelmingly so.

At dinner, Grandpa K started asking questions about the plans for calving. "So, is Alyssa here ready to solo, or are you going to keep her joined at the hip with you, Beau?"

Beau nodded. "Alyssa is ready, she's studied everything and knows the herd as well as anyone. I haven't seen her in a critical situation but hopefully the two of us will be able to work together on any of those that come up. It's always better to have two trained vets work together, but all of you are capable of assisting if we need to be separated. Just make sure to keep your cell phones charged and call as needed. For non-emergencies, group text is good."

Emma said, "I have Tony pre-enrolled at the daycare in town, if you think you might need me, and all my book-keeping clients are up to date and capable of waiting a couple of weeks, if we're too busy on the weekends."

"That's great, Emma sweetheart, but hopefully my grandson will be able to stay home with his mama. We have a couple extra hands hired and with Alyssa being almost grad-uated that will help with any troubles we run into." Travis winked at Tony. Tony waived to his papa.

Meg said, "We can trade off watching Tony. I would be happy to stay with that little cutie rather than being out with the animals, at least part of the time."

Emma laughed. "I'll take you up on that, mom. I love calving season—all the new life springing forth."

Beau said dryly, "Yeah the first fifty or so I agree with you." He shrugged. "After that it just gets monotonous."

Alyssa slowly turned her head and looked at him. "I've never done more than a hundred calves, you do three times that. The last few years dad's increased production for the tourist influx, but I've been at school here in Colorado and missed the spring calving. Oh boy, I might have some culture shock."

Beau grinned at her. "Like I said the first fifty are special, after that it's the same thing over and over and over and over and over."

Cade patted her hand. "Stick with me kid and I'll show you the ropes."

Alyssa rolled her eyes at his stupid brother. He might have to pound some sense into Cade if he didn't stop flirting with Alyssa. It set his blood to boil every single time and he wanted to knock him into next week. Alyssa didn't appear to encourage the flirtation, but it still made him half crazy. He narrowed his eyes at his brother who grinned at him. Cade was skating on thin ice and appeared to enjoy taunting him, which ticked him off.

He stood and threw his napkin down. "I'm going to go check on Dolly and the preemie."

"But we haven't had pie yet," his mother said.

"I'll get some later."

"Do you need my help?" Alyssa asked.

Beau growled. "No, stay here and flirt with my idiot brother."

Alyssa frowned and Cade grinned and Beau stomped out of the house as he heard his mother say, "What's that all about?"

$\sim$

ALYSSA WAITED a few moments and then excused herself and

followed Beau out to the animals. She was boiling mad and going to give that man a piece of her mind.

Beau turned toward her as she walked into the birthing barn. "I told you, I don't need you."

"Yeah, I heard you." She walked right up to him and poked him in the chest with one finger. The man was hard as a rock; he had muscles on top of muscles. "I thought you were done acting like a dumb ass. What was that comment about me flirting with your brother? I don't deserve it, and I don't appreciate it. Just what in the hell is wrong with you? Cade is teasing me like he does your sister. It's not flirting, you big jerk."

"Well, you might not see it as flirting, but it is."

"Bull shit. Cade is pushing your buttons and you're letting him. And for the life of me I can't figure out why in the hell you give a crap about his comments. He's got nothing on you —you're older,"—*poke*—"and smarter,"—*poke*—"and sexier,"—*poke*—"than he'll ever be, so stop acting like an ass." On that, she smacked him in the chest with the heel of her hand because her finger hurt from poking his steel-like muscles.

She watched as a slow grin slid over his face. "You think I'm sexier than Cade?"

"Oh, for God's sake, is that all you heard? Yes, you're sexier, but you're also a dumb ass and a jerk and just a plain ass. And, apparently, an idiot too." She fumed and then turned to march away from the idiot standing there grinning at her. How in the world did humanity survive with men being as stupid as the one in the barn with her? She just didn't know. Why hadn't a bear or lion or dinosaur have eaten them long ago? What was wrong with natural selection anyway?

She was halfway to the door when Beau called out.

"Alyssa, wait."

She stopped but didn't turn—she didn't want to see his stupid, sexy face.

He spoke right behind her. "I'm sorry, Alyssa. I don't know what it is about you, but every comment any of my brothers make about you just makes me see red."

She slowly turned toward him. "Why is that Beau? It doesn't mean anything."

He rubbed his hand over the back of his neck. "I don't know, but it makes me crazy. I mean, you're just an intern and too young, and you live hundreds of miles away. So, nothing can come of this, but I just can't stand to hear my brother flirting with you."

Every word from his mouth deflated her. *Just an intern. Too young.* And the real kicker, lived too far away. Like she wasn't worth a two-day drive. Like a person couldn't move. What a lame excuse. Fine, idiot. "Well, get over it. If you aren't interested, then you don't get to dictate who is. You're just my *old* teacher this semester, Beau. So, stop acting like a dog in heat."

CHAPTER 10

*A*lyssa and Beau kept their interaction on a purely professional level as the first wave of babies came into the world. He was leery of her and she was pissed at him, so it worked out fine. They split up to work both the pastured mothers and the birthing stalls. They traded places at lunch, so Beau could make sure everything was going well. She was glad to be out in the fresh air part of the day, also. Cade and Chase took the evening rounds and Travis and Grandpa K took early mornings, saying they'd been getting up before the sun their whole lives and why would they stop now. The graveyard shift was mostly completed by the hired hands. But, if anyone on any shift needed a vet to assist, they called or texted both Alyssa and Beau.

One night at two in the morning, Alyssa vaguely heard her phone chime with an incoming text, she reached out to check it and knocked it onto the floor. Before she could reach it, there was a sharp knock on her door. Beau called her name, so she left the phone where it was and hurried to the door.

She opened it to see Beau pulling on a shirt, his pants still unbuttoned—and if she hadn't been worried about what the problem was she might have drooled. But, clearly, something was wrong.

"We've got an emergency. Can you grab some clothes and meet me downstairs? We'll need to take the truck out to the pasture, so you can pull them on as I drive."

"Of course, I'm right behind you."

He nodded. "I'll bring your boots and coat, just put something on your feet to get to the truck."

"Got it." She turned and didn't even shut her bedroom door as she started grabbing clothes. The sports bra she slept in would do, and she could pull her jeans on over her sleep shorts, her long sleep shirt would have to go, so she grabbed a normal T-shirt and a flannel shirt, socks, her phone, and her hair brush—because she knew she had bed head and couldn't stand the idea of not at least running a brush through her locks and slapping it into a pony tail. And her breath mints—always good to have mints in your pocket. She stuck her feet into some rain boots and hustled down the stairs.

Beau had the truck pulled up to the back door, engine running and passenger side open. Alyssa clambered in and shut the door as Beau took off.

"What's happening? I dropped my phone and haven't seen the text yet." Alyssa yanked off her sleep shirt and pulled on the t-shirt she'd brought.

Beau glanced her way. "One of the dams is hemorrhaging. I just hope we make it in time to stop the bleeding, so we don't lose her."

She pulled on her jeans over her sleep shorts and lifted her rear up to get them over her hips and zipped. "Is she done giving birth?"

"Yeah, at least that's not another problem to deal with. The baby is fine."

"Good." She pulled on her socks and boots. Then, snapped on her seatbelt to keep her from bouncing all over the damn truck. Alyssa ran the brush through her hair and yanked it up into a quick tail and popped in a breath mint. "Want a mint?"

"God, yes. Thanks."

Yanking on her flannel shirt, she tied it at the waist rather than trying to get it tucked into her jeans, as Beau's truck careened its way across the pasture. He was trying not to frighten the cattle, but driving as quickly as possible. She'd put her jacket on when they got out of the truck, if she needed it.

"There they are." She pointed to the left just as Beau jerked the truck in that direction.

"Yep. I'm going to pull in to the left a little, so we have two sets of headlights illuminating the area from a couple of angles."

"Good idea."

They got out of the truck and grabbed the medical supplies from the back seat.

"About damn time you got here," one of the hired hands, Carlos, said.

"They don't make transporters yet, we got here as quick as we could." Beau moved in to see what was going on and Alyssa followed him.

John, the older man, said, "We did everything we could think of to stop the bleeding and it's slowed down some, but not enough."

"I'm sure you did everything just fine," Alyssa said. "Sometimes births cause a vein to get severed or there's a tear in the uterus. Don't worry, one of you hold her so she doesn't jerk and the other can keep the herd back and tend to the calf, so we can work." Beau was too busy working on the heifer to comment on their behavior, but

58

Alyssa knew that half of being a vet was reassuring the humans.

≈

BEAU VAGUELY HEARD Alyssa talking to the two ranch hands. He was relieved she was doing it, so he could work on the dam. It really was convenient to have two vets on a ranch.

Beau put the long glove on, that Alyssa had handed him before he asked. "I see it—there's a vaginal tear. Get me some sutures Alyssa."

He hadn't finished speaking before she handed him the pre-threaded sutures. Yep, damn handy to have her.

Beau took her offering and carefully reached inside the cow, keeping a visual eye on the place that needed repair as much as he could but a lot of it would have to be done by feel. It wasn't easy because there wasn't much room, but he managed. He also had some gauze to dab at the blood when it got too bad for him to see the tear. Only being able to have one hand inside the animal had caused him to get creative so he used gauze secured to the back of his hand.

When he finished stitching, he got some clean gauze from Alyssa and mopped up the blood still inside to make sure there weren't any other bleeders. There were none, so he assessed the animal to see if she had lost too much blood.

"I think she'll be fine, but let's get her and the calf in the truck so I can take them back to the ranch."

"We haven't weighed the calf or tagged him. We noticed right away the dam was bleeding too much and that took all our focus. Sorry, boss." John shrugged.

Beau and Alyssa both shook their heads. Beau said, "Nope, you did exactly the right thing, we can weigh and tag the little guy in the stall."

They got the cattle loaded and Alyssa patted John and

Carlos both on the shoulder, murmuring encouragement to them both. Then, she climbed into the truck after looking at the cattle one last time.

"She's cleaning him, so they should be fine," she reported, as she shut the door.

"Good to know." Beau started slowly across the pasture taking the easiest path for his cargo. Since disaster was averted images of Alyssa earlier—looking so cute and rumpled when she opened the door to him—assailed him. Then, ripping off her top and pulling on her clothes right next to him. The images were not real clear, but evocative anyway. He needed to get his mind off her and with a quickness.

"You did good out there, anticipating my needs. Thanks. It went a lot faster with the two of us. I was thinking it would be handy to have two medically trained people all the time."

CHAPTER 11

*A*lyssa flushed with pleasure at his praise. Was he suggesting she stay on at their ranch? It wasn't her plan to do so, but maybe she should think about it. It was a great working environment.

Beau continued speaking. "I wonder if anyone around here would be interested in taking some classes to become my right hand."

Oh, so he wasn't hinting at her staying, just thinking out loud. Well, fine. She had other plans, anyway. But she felt oddly deflated that he wasn't wanting *her* to stay. It was a silly idea anyway; her family would miss her—especially her father, who whined incessantly about her being so far away as it was. Still, Beau could at least want her to stay even if she couldn't.

"Alyssa?"

What, she wasn't good enough? Did he just think good vets just grew on trees? Like she didn't have anything special, and they could just train anyone to have her skills and compassion. Well she didn't think it worked that way. She knew she was good at what she did, and if Beau couldn't see it? Screw him. Stupid man.

"Alyssa?"

"What? You think my expertise can be learned by anyone? I don't think so." She turned to look out the window and folded her arms over her chest.

"What are you talking about? Alyssa, I was just saying how much I appreciated you being there tonight. You handled the ranch hands really well and anticipated my needs, and well, I am damn thankful it was you by my side tonight."

"Oh, well, you're welcome. I'm here to work after all."

Beau groaned. "Are you ever going to let me live that down?"

She smiled sweetly. "Nope, I have no intention whatsoever of letting you live that down." Men, in her experience, needed a little humility dumped over their head, on a regular basis—*especially Beau*—and she was happy to do the dumping.

∼

BEAU HAD no idea what had just happened as they were driving back, but he'd learned—at a young age—never to question a woman when her mind seemed to have veered from the conversation. He had a mother and a sister, and both sometimes said things that seemed off the wall, and the few times he had questioned them about it, they had gone off on him. Finally, his father had taken him aside and told him just to let strange statements go—that if the woman wanted to elaborate she would, and if she didn't, he was just asking for trouble if he pursued it. Unless a woman said everything was *fine*… and then you started with flowers and an apology, whether you knew what you were apologizing for or not.

They got back to the calving barn and unloaded the animals. It did appear that the calf had been nursing, and that all was fine and dandy in the animal world. The mother was a little shaky, but her eyes were clear and focused, so he thought she would be good. He didn't want to give her any blood or an IV if he didn't need to.

They got the animals settled. Alyssa sighed. "It looks like they'll both be okay. Don't you think?"

"Yep, I agree. We'll keep an eye on her, but I don't think we need to worry. We've got a few hours before our shift if you want to go grab some more sleep."

"I could use a bit more." She yawned and then nodded.

"Don't forget to get your stuff out of the truck." He didn't want to stumble upon any of it later when his defenses were down. Especially her sleep shirt. Yeah, no reminders of her in just her bra, thank you very much. That was not something he wanted to dwell on. Or her shimmying into her jeans. Or her slender bare feet. Nope, no reminders.

"I'll grab it on the way in. Good job out there," she said over her shoulder, as she started toward the door.

He saluted and looked back at the cattle, or at least pretended to, as he watched her walk away. She had a fine ass, and the shirt tied at her waist made him think of untying it and shoving her up against the barn wall. Nope, not a good idea. He needed to record what had happened in the field. Work was the answer, not fantasizing about the hot woman.

On her way back to bed.

Alone.

He rubbed his hand down his face and walked to the workstation they had in the birthing barn. Work. Work. Work.

He had just finished logging all the data into the computer when his dad walked in. He set one of the travel cups of coffee he held on the desk. "Heard you had some trouble this morning."

Beau picked up the mug and took a long drink of the life-giving elixir. He'd been dragging, and this would help. "Yeah a vaginal tear. Got it stitched up. I think she'll be fine. No trouble with the calf."

"Good. We'll need to check the dam later, to see if it's wise to breed her again."

"Of course, thanks for the coffee."

"You bet. Figured you would need some about now. How'd Alyssa do?" His dad settled one hip on the desk.

Beau's mind whipped back to her yanking her clothes off in the front seat of his truck. He took another drink of coffee to get his brain and body back under control. "She did great. Anticipated my every need. Her being there made everything so much smoother and quicker. I barely had to think what I needed next and she was handing it to me. She's quite the asset."

"I kind of figured that. Her father called me last night to ask how she's doing." He laughed. "Concerned fathers. Especially fathers and their daughters. I'm also guilty in that respect."

Beau grinned at his dad. He was a rough and tumble cowboy, but he had a soft spot for his daughter. He'd about gone crazy when she'd turned up pregnant, with no baby daddy. But Emma had talked him down. Beau guessed his mother probably had had a hand in calming his father, too. "You told him she was doing good, right?"

"Yep. Told him she's a great help. Haven't seen any evidence to the contrary and I have only had good reports from everyone." He shook his head. "Well, better get to it. Your grandfather will be chewing me out if I dawdle too long. Daylight's burning."

Beau looked out at the pitch black. "Not yet, it isn't."

His dad barked out a laugh. "Your grandfather has a different opinion. He can see a tiny ray of light and believe it's full sun."

"Yep, even if it's from a flashlight."

"You got that right. Later."

"See ya."

Beau sat there for a minute thinking about family—both he and Alyssa were from close-knit families. Ranch families often were. He figured her father missed her and Beau realized he was going to feel the same, when she was gone. She had a way of lighting up the room and putting everyone at ease, and her veterinary skills couldn't be beat. Yeah, he was going to miss her when she left them to go back to her life. *Well, hell.*

CHAPTER 12

*I*t was time to call her family. Alyssa had been remiss about talking to them and she missed them. Most days were fine but today she just needed to see their faces. She waited until she knew they would all be around the dinner table. Normally, they had a no-cell-phones-at-the-table rule, but she'd let her step mom, Ellen, know she was going to call tonight. She touched the Face-time app and connected to her step mom's phone.

"Hi, everybody." The phone was pointed out at the table and being swiveled so she could see each one and they could see her.

Her dad said, "It's about damn time you called in, young lady. You can't be that busy."

"Oh, daddy! I miss you, too. But we have been pretty busy. They have three hundred pregnant mommas here."

Ten-year-old Lance said, "Three hundred pregnant? Really? That's almost as many as our whole herd."

"Yes, little brother, it's quite a bit larger ranch than ours."

"With three times the problems, I would guess." Her oldest brother Mike said.

She laughed. "You're right about that, Mikey. We've had a preemie, a bleeder, and a ProtectiveMama. Plus, one of the older non-pregnant heifers got caught in a leg hold beaver trap that was on the land illegally."

"Damn poachers," Mike said.

"Exactly. We've got the first wave of two-year-olds in birthing stalls along with a couple of others. One that loves the river a little too much. They call her River PITA."

Thirteen-year-old Beth laughed. "For river pain in the ass. That's a hoot."

Ellen turned the phone toward herself. "How is the family treating you Alyssa?"

"They've been great, mom. It's a houseful, they've got a set of twins, too, a couple of years older than me." She wasn't about to tell them about Beau's reception. "I'm learning a lot from the vet. He's the second oldest son and good at what he does." Not to mention sexy as hell, but again, something she wasn't going to mention. "Where's Tim?"

They all said in unison, "At the art gallery."

"Of course." She should have remembered that; he'd been working there in the evenings for nearly five years. "Tell him I said hi. Now, go around the table and tell me one thing that's happened that I missed." It was a long-standing tradition in their house to give each person a time to share and she loved it.

Lance told her all about a science project he was working on. Vance told her about his baseball team starting practice soon. Beth talked about the newest graphic novel that had been published. About four years ago, she'd cajoled their local children's book author into creating a character named Beth, who was a heroine in the graphic novels he was just starting to write. He was still producing them and allowed Beth to participate in the plotting and beta reading. The adults caught her up on ranch business and home life.

When each person had spoken she had tears threatening. So, she told them she loved them and would call again soon. Her father's voice was gruff when he said goodbye. Damn. Now she missed them even more.

It was still early. Maybe she should go spend some time with Tony and Emma. That might get her out of her funk. Staying alone in her room would only make it worse. She left her room in a hurry and went in search of mother and son. She found them in the family room.

"I need some Tony time."

Emma smiled. "Really? That's awesome. I need to run into town for an hour or two. One of my clients needs me to sort out her finances. Tony would love to have you help watch him. Mom is out with Dad. Two watchers are better than one, so if you could help that would make me feel so much better."

"Sure, I would be happy to." She looked at Tony. "Want to play with me tonight?"

Tony nodded and came over to her.

As Tony climbed into her lap, Emma said, "Alyssa, that is just spectacular. I made a list of his activities and if you wouldn't mind hanging out in my room with him, once he goes to bed, that would ease my mind. My brother has good intentions, but men are not built the same as a woman. None of my brothers have been fathers yet, so they are great on the playing with him side, but not so great at the putting to bed and comforting side."

"I understand." That would keep her occupied and not feeling sorry for herself for a few hours. Perfect.

"Great, I'm going to go then, he'll be here in a minute or two. Here's the list and a bag of snacks." Emma handed her the items and was out the door.

Alyssa started to wonder which brother she had just committed to spend the evening with when she heard

Emma talking to someone in the hall. "Alyssa is going to help you and hang out with you when you put Tony to bed. The two of you will be great. Thanks so much, big brother."

Just before he walked in the room, Alyssa realized it had to be Beau. The twins were out on pasture patrol, Drew was on swing shift this week, and she'd seen Adam dressed up and walking out the door when she'd come looking for Emma. Damn, just what she didn't need. To spend all that time with the man. She'd been trying to avoid him in the evenings. She already spent a good portion of the day with him and she liked it a little too much, so she was trying to distance herself.

"So, we're co-babysitting tonight?" His deep voice sent skitters of pleasure through her. He looked good with his five o'clock shadow darkening his chin. He'd obviously showered, his hair was damp, and he had on a black T-shirt and dark jeans. She wanted to lap him right up.

She nodded. "It appears so. I just needed a little Tony time and Emma was thrilled I could help you baby sit."

"Why did you need Tony time?"

Did she want to tell him the truth? Not really, but she couldn't think up another story quick enough, so the truth it was going to be. "I talked to my family tonight and was feeling a little homesick."

"I can understand that. How is their calving coming along?"

"Good, actually. Hey. What happens with Tony if there is an emergency with one of the animals?"

"We call Emma and she starts back and Grandpa K is here if we need him to pinch hit for the time it takes her to drive home."

Tony put his hand on her face. "Lyssa, we play *Chutes and Ladders*?"

Alyssa looked down at the little boy on her lap. "Sure, we can do that, Tony."

Beau grinned. "I'll get it."

Trying to ignore the hot man, Alyssa said to the child, "Your mom left some snacks too."

Tony clapped his hands, his eyes sparkling. "Snacks."

Alyssa laughed. The little boy was adorable and just what she needed.

~

BEAU COULDN'T BELIEVE his luck. He'd been trying to avoid Alyssa for the last few days. They already had to work together whenever one of the cattle needed both of them, and even when they didn't, she reported to him every night what had happened on her shift. So, that was plenty of inter-action—if he just could get his mind to stop flashing pictures of her half naked in his truck. It was ridiculous, and he had decided the only way to handle it was to be a bit more removed.

But here she was, and she clearly needed to have some time to play with Tony. She'd looked so lonely and vulner-able when she said she was homesick. He would never deny her time with his nephew. And he wasn't about to renege on his promise to Emma to watch Tony. The only reason he would do that was for an emergency. So, it looked like he was spending the evening with Alyssa.

He just hoped the children's game would keep him from lusting after the woman. But she needed to stop laughing, because that sound sent fire racing through his blood. He went across the room to the game closet and got out the game that was Tony's favorite at the moment.

Alyssa was digging through the snack bag with Tony. She looked so natural with his nephew on her lap, he was shocked when a wave of longing swept through him. He'd never yearned for a child before, but just looking at Alyssa with the little boy on her lap did strange things to him. Nope not going there, had he lost his mind? He pushed those wayward feelings into a box and locked the lid. Then put a chain around it with a huge padlock, buried it deep, and finally—just to make sure—he covered it with barbed wire.

Beau shook his head and started setting up the game while Alyssa and Tony finished deciding on the snacks. They each had a juice box, which to him, tasted more like water than juice, but it made Tony happy to share, so he would drink it. They had little cups filled with cheese puffs that had slightly more taste and some cookies that looked like *Fig Newtons* but had strawberry filling.

They ate their snacks and played two rousing games of Chutes and Ladders. Amazingly enough, Tony won both games with only a little help from the adults. But then the little boy started to fade.

Alyssa said, "Tony, let's get you in your PJs and then Beau and I will read you a story."

"'Kay, Lyssa." Tony looked at him. "Horsey back, Uncle B?"

"Sure thing, pardner." Beau took the little guy and put him on his back where he gripped onto Beau's shirt with both hands. Beau held onto Tony's feet, bent over slightly, and neighed.

Tony laughed, and Beau shook a bit, making the little guy squeal with laughter, and started out the door toward Emma's room.

CHAPTER 13

*A*lyssa followed the two guys out of the room and had a nice view of Beau's ass as he bent over to give his nephew a horsey ride. It was a very excellent sight to behold. *No lusting after the cowboy, Alyssa. He's your boss, woman. Knock it off, already.* What was it with her and this man? She didn't have this uncontrollable lust with the rest of the good-looking men on the ranch—just Beau. And now that he was treating her with respect and even some admiration she had to admit she was falling for him, a little. She knew it couldn't, shouldn't, wouldn't go anywhere. But she was not going to lie to herself. She fantasized about it going somewhere—more often than she would ever admit.

When they got to Emma's room she asked, "Does he need a bath before bed?"

Tony slid off Beau's back to the floor. "No, Emma said she'd given him one earlier when Grandpa K had taken him out in the yard. Apparently, they found some mud."

She laughed. "Yeah, that would bring bath time on early, wouldn't it?"

Tony clapped his hands. "Mud, mud, mud. Very dirty mud."

They both laughed at the boy.

She said, "PJ time and then story."

"PJ time story, Lyssa."

She looked at Beau. "Is there a PJ story?"

"I have no idea."

Tony hopped over to his bookshelf and pulled out a story —and yes, it was about PJs and animals dancing. She laughed. "Alrighty then, PJs first and PJ story second."

Tony nodded then looked at his uncle. "*G'night Moon*, Uncle B?"

Beau shook his head. "I think we're getting scammed here, but yes, I'll get that book, too."

They read the stories to Tony and he was asleep before Beau could finish all of his. Alyssa tucked the covers in around him and kissed his forehead. She looked up and saw Beau watching her with the oddest expression. It looked like lust and longing and she didn't know what else, but she wasn't going to let it slide this time. "What?"

He shook his head, turned abruptly, and put both books back into the bookshelf. She waited by the door for him to come out and gently closed it almost all the way. Emma had two adjoining rooms—one for Tony and another for herself. She turned to find Beau looking out the dark window like he could see something.

"Beau, what's wrong?" She walked up next to him and put her hand on his back.

⮑

HE TURNED SLOWLY from the window. "You're a danger, Alyssa."

"I'm a danger? How do you figure that?" Alyssa looked at

him like he'd lost his mind. And she was right. He'd lost his mind after the first step she'd taken on the ranch.

"You're a danger to me. You're too smart. Too beautiful. And too young."

"Pffft, age is just a number, Beau. You're only a few years older than I am."

He shook his head. "No seven years is too big of a span. You're just barely an adult."

"I am twenty-two and I know my own mind and heart." She poked him in the chest. "So, quit being a chicken-shit, cowboy."

Yeah, she was right about that he was scared to fricken death over his feelings for her. She had another year or two of college to get her master's degree. She would make a helluva asset with a reproduction specialization. She was already a great vet assistant, but once she got her masters or if she continued on to get her DVM or PhD, she could write her own ticket. So, he refused to let his feelings show. Beau couldn't, wouldn't derail her education. He forced his feet to take a step back, out of the danger zone.

Alyssa growled and grabbed him by the front of his shirt and dragged him back to her. She fisted his hair and pulled his mouth down to hers. And he was lost. Lost in the heat. Lost in the taste. Just lost. So, he kissed her back. He kissed her like there was no tomorrow. He kissed her like she wasn't leaving. He kissed her like she would always be his. But she wouldn't be his—she was leaving, and there was a tomorrow. So, he broke the kiss and pulled back slowly, out of the heat, away from the taste, to find himself panting. She was panting too. He leaned his forehead on hers. "We can't. This isn't meant to be."

She looked so sad when she asked, "Why? Why isn't it meant to be, Beau?"

He didn't get the chance to answer. A cacophony of

yelling and stomping boot heels rang out. Drew was hollering at the top of his lungs.

"Beau! Beau! Where the hell are you?"

He sighed and opened the door. "Keep it down, dumbass, you're going to wake up Tony."

Drew grimaced. "Oh, sorry, I forgot. But you have to come quick. We think we have a lead on the trappers. We're going to get up a search party tonight and see if we can round them up. Can you come with us?"

Beau looked back at Alyssa standing where he'd left her, looking so beautiful with swollen lips and high color in her cheeks. Her hair was coming out of its fastenings and she looked love struck. He wanted to stay with her.

She motioned for him to go. "I'll be fine. I can watch Tony sleep and I'll call Grandpa K if there are any animal emergencies. You go with Drew. Good luck."

He turned back to his brother and nodded. "All right, let's go get them—so none of the other animals get caught in their traps."

Drew turned and started down the hall. Beau followed him, but when the door snicked closed, he wondered if he'd just made the biggest mistake of his life.

CHAPTER 14

*B*eau talked to himself all the way to the mud room. He couldn't turn down his brother's request for help, but it was the worst possible time to leave Alyssa. He needed to explain what he meant. He didn't want her to think she wasn't desirable. She was the most fascinating and wonderful woman he'd ever known, but she had commitments and family and so did he.

As Beau pulled on his boots and coat, Drew filled him in on what he knew. "Don and Jim Johnson were headed out to do some fishing at the river late this afternoon. They parked in the old campground and saw another truck already there. They were surprised to see anyone else parking there, since it's closed, but figured maybe others were going fishing too. When they got close to the river they saw some guys near the beaver dams in the northeast pasture. When the other guys looked up Don waived, like you do. But then the other guys just left, in a hurry, heading back toward the campground.

"The Johnsons didn't think much of it and went about fishing until they heard a snap and a beaver started screaming. They went into the pasture, toward the sound, and found a trapped beaver near where the other guys had been. They managed to set it free and it didn't seem to be too damaged, so they called the station and we went out to investigate. We found a couple of other traps near the beaver ponds.

"Jim was pretty observant and had plenty of information about the truck and the guys. The description jogged an officer's memory who had seen a similar truck coming onto our land up north off and on, the last few weeks. He'd thought maybe it was a hired hand he didn't know."

"But it's not one of our guys, is it." Beau grabbed a couple of flashlights off the shelf, checked to make sure they worked —as in, had fresh batteries.

"Nope, so I got to thinking maybe they are camping on our land. Since we're busy with calving season, it would be pretty easy to lay low in one of the northern pastures. Adam and some other officers are going to meet us where the truck's been seen, and we can spread out from there. We don't have enough officers to double up, which is why we're taking you and Adam, and a couple of the hired hands from town. Since we think it's our land they're on, it's logical to use people familiar with the territory. That way, we can have an officer and a civilian per team."

"Makes sense." Beau took a small first aid kit, just in case. He knew the officers were armed so he didn't bring a rifle. He didn't want to spook the guys and start a shootout; rifles were pretty obvious and could be seen as threatening.

They got into Drew's patrol vehicle and headed out to see if they could catch the poachers.

∾

ALYSSA WATCHED the guys drive off to find the illegal trappers. She knew he had to go, but couldn't it have waited five minutes? That kiss had been spectacular—off the charts—and then he'd pulled back and said it wasn't meant to be. What wasn't meant to be? The kiss? A relationship? A fling? Certainly not forever—there were too many obstacles to forever. Maybe that's all he'd meant and while her head might agree with that assessment, her heart was not on board. Her heart, it seemed, wanted Beau and didn't care about logistics. Her body was right there with her heart, ready and willing to take on the challenges.

She didn't have a lot of experience with sex, but she knew enough to know that the feelings she had experienced with Beau were exceptional. He'd set her whole body on fire with just his lips and tongue. His hands hadn't moved one inch. But every bit of her was still tingling—even now. The man could kiss. She wanted more of those kisses. If truth be told she wanted to strip him naked and revel in all that warm male flesh. But was that a good idea?

Probably not. Why did her brain have to go all logical on her? Yes, they lived in different states. Yes, she had another year of school left. Yes, her father wanted her back working for him once she got her master's degree. He had ideas for increasing production; the town had grown a lot in the last few years and the demand for beef had risen to the point that they were having trouble keeping up. Of course, people could order beef from the Safeway in Chelan, but her father, and his father before him, had always kept their little town supplied. It was probably more a point of pride than anything else, but her dad wanted to explore some options, and he hoped her specialized study would help him decide the best way to go. He'd probably read a million articles on the subject and she didn't know what else she would be able to contribute, but she would give it a try. She was excited that he wanted her opinion—maybe he didn't still think of her as an eight-year-old.

Alyssa sighed. Yes, she certainly had lots of reasons why this thing with Beau would never work out. But her heart and body vehemently disagreed. They wanted Beau any way they could get him. All she had to do was figure out whether to try to get him, or avoid him—to keep her heart from getting more involved with the man. He was a good guy and her heart was already sold on him.

She realized she was still standing in front of the window staring sightlessly down the driveway. She turned and went to the rocking chair in the room. But what was she supposed to do now? Maybe text her best friend Rachel, she was always a good sounding board. She looked at the time and subtracted the hour time difference. Plenty early.

> *Alyssa: Hey Rachel, got time to chat?*
> *Rachel: You bet, how's it going?*
> *Alyssa: Great actually. Been busy. Learning a lot.*
> *Rachel: How's Mr. Cranky Pants treating you?*
> *Alyssa: Beau was having a bad day I guess. He's been great since.*
> *Rachel: Really? Well good I'm glad he got over himself.*
> *Alyssa: Yeah, he's been great to work with, compliments and everything.*
> *Rachel: How could he not, you're awesome!*
> *Alyssa: Thanks BFF. So, about the man in question.*
> *Rachel: Yeeeessss?*
> *Alyssa: I may have kissed him.*
> *Rachel: What? Calling right now.*

Alyssa answered her phone before it rang.

Rachel squealed in her ear. "What do you mean you may have kissed him? Isn't he like ten years older than you? And mean to boot?"

"*Shhh*, not so loud. I'm watching Tony and you're going to wake him with all that shouting. Even if I am in the next room."

"Fine. I'll lower my voice, but what did you expect from me? You kissed your boss or teacher or whatever he is. Have you lost your mind? Did he kiss you back? Was it wonderful or awful? I need more information here."

Alyssa laughed. "Do you want those answered in order?"

"Hell no. Start with the end and work backwards."

"It was amazingly wonderful. Yes, he kissed me back. It is quite possible I have lost my mind. Or at least my heart. But then, he pulled back and said it wasn't meant to be." It made her sad again even to say the words out loud.

"WTF. What wasn't meant to be? The kiss? A relationship?" Rachel demanded.

"I have no idea. His brother came screaming down the hall wanting Beau to go help him hunt some illegal trappers."

"And he just left you high and dry?" she squeaked.

Alyssa defended him. "He didn't have a choice."

"Sure, he did. He could tell his brother no."

"Not really. A cow Beau raised from birth got caught in one of their traps a few weeks ago, so Beau has a vested interest and it's a lot of land to search," Alyssa explained even though she kind of agreed with Rachel.

"Well, damn. So, that's why you called me? To take your mind off it or talk it out?"

"I didn't call. I texted. You called."

Rachel giggled. "Well, of course I did. You can't text someone about a hot kiss and not expect a phone call to get the deets."

Alyssa laughed. "I suppose you're right. I just needed my best friend."

"Aw, I love you, too. Now, what are we going to do about Mr. Kiss-and-Run?"

Alyssa laughed again; she really did need Rachel. "No clue."

"I guess the real question is what do you want to do? Kiss him again? Have sex with him? Get married and have his babies? Just where are you on the spectrum of boy-meets-girl?"

"I haven't quite figured that out, yet." She sighed. "I mean, more kisses would be good. My body would be happy to have sex with him. But my mind keeps telling me all the reasons this is a bad idea."

"Like what?" Rachel asked.

"Well, he's seven years older than me."

"That's just a number. Who cares?"

"He lives in Colorado and I live in Washington."

"That's just geography, you've been in Colorado for four years now and are planning at least one more."

Alyssa got up and walked to the window. "Yeah, but what happens after that? What if my heart picks him to be my one and only?"

"Hmm. Well, you could stay in Colorado and make me and your whole family miss you. Or, he could move to Washington."

She shook her head even though Rachel couldn't see it. "And make his whole family miss him? Plus, he's needed here. They've got too big of a herd to not have a vet on staff. At least half of the year, anyway."

"Well, hell. That is a conundrum. But you don't have to decide all that today. Do you? Maybe he sucks in bed—you should sleep with him and find out." Rachel said firmly.

Alyssa groaned. "Now there is a ridiculous idea. Sleep with him in the hopes that he sucks in bed and then I wouldn't have to worry about the future."

Rachel laughed. "Or maybe he would be so good you

would forget all about us and follow him anywhere, so to speak."

"God, I've missed talking to you."

"Back at you. You could call me once in a while." Rachel huffed.

"Yeah, I've just been working hard and studying the birthing records at night—so I will be ready for anything."

"Of course, you have been, Little Miss Over Achiever. But you could take fifteen minutes and call your best friend. At least a couple times a week."

"You're right, and I will." Alyssa decided.

"Especially after you implement your plan with Mr. Hottie."

Alyssa laughed. "First, I have to figure out the plan. Then, it's a promise. Love you."

"Love you back."

Alyssa was happy Rachel had called. She didn't know what she wanted to do about Beau, but talking to Rachel had given her some insights into her own heart and mind that she needed. When the knob to the door turned, her breath caught before she realized it couldn't be Beau back so soon.

Emma walked in and smiled. "I heard in town that they had some clues about the poachers, so I came back. I'd already found the glitch and fixed it, so it was easy to leave. I'll need to go back and finish up the records in a day or two, but they are good to go, for now. How was Tony?"

"He was great. We played *Chutes and Ladders* and then read him two books. He didn't quite make it through the second one."

"Two books?" Emma's eyebrows shot up.

"Yeah one from me and one from Beau."

"Oh, so he played you rookies." Motherly amusement showed on her face.

"I had a feeling he was doing that, but we were happy to indulge him."

"Yeah, occasionally doesn't hurt."

Alyssa asked, "So, you know Beau went with Drew, out to see if they can find the trappers?"

"I figured he would. He's not one to sit idle when they found clues, and someone said they were needing some help to search our land. So, it makes sense."

"I hope they're careful," Alyssa said.

"No worries about that—they know the land and will be smart about it. If they do find the guys."

"Good. Well, I think I'll go study up on the next round of births."

"Thanks for watching Tony, and don't worry about the guys."

As Alyssa walked down the hall toward her room, she decided she wasn't worried about the guys getting hurt—but she was worried about one guy in particular. And what she wanted to do with him.

CHAPTER 15

*D*rew drove slowly onto the land where they thought the trappers might be. He'd turned off his lights when they exited the main road, and they were travelling by moonlight. Fortunately, it was a bright night with no clouds. "Turn your text notification to silent. We'll communicate with the other teams that way. If anyone finds them, we'll let the others know so we can close in on them. When everyone is in place, we'll all walk in at the same time, so they won't try anything stupid."

Beau did as he was told, thinking if the poachers had any light at the camp this idea would work fine. If not, they might see the cell screens light up and get spooked. But, it was a better idea than going in alone or having no communication.

They parked the truck and started to walk their designated section of land. They knew which areas they could avoid because of dense foliage. The northeast pasture had a couple of camping areas they used occasionally, when they needed to stay out with the herd for some reason. There were also camping spots in two of the other quadrants the hired hands were checking. A small cabin was in the north-west pasture Adam and the officer he was with would be hitting. Everything was silent except for the night animals and bugs. They were chirping away as normal, so that was a good sign that nothing dangerous was going on.

About twenty minutes in, his cell vibrated and he looked at the screen.

> Adam: They're in the cabin and they're either drunk or high because they are singing up a storm. We could have brought tanks and they wouldn't notice.
> Drew: We're the farthest out. We'll go get the vehicle and drive it in so we don't have to carry their asses out.
> Adam: Perfect. We'll be waiting.

Drew and Beau hotfooted it back to the SUV and started it up. They used the lights to connect to the dirt road that would take them toward the cabin, but Drew turned them off before they rounded the trees that would allow a visual to the area. He got within a couple dozen yards before he shut it down and parked.

It was a tiny cabin with only one door and two windows. The hired hand teams were at the windows and Adam and Sheriff Carlson were waiting by the door. Beau and Drew joined them, and they prepared to enter. When Drew opened the door a waft of pot smoke engulfed them. The officers went in first, guns drawn, and Adam and Beau followed. As soon as they saw the guys inside the officers dropped their weapons to their sides. The guys hadn't even noticed the four of them were in the room yet, they were so wasted. One of them was tall and skinny with long greasy blond hair. He was singing off key so loud, Beau cringed. The other was shorter and more muscular with a buzz cut. He seemed to be able to carry a tune, not that he could be heard over Greasy Hair.

Beau looked around and there was evidence everywhere that these were the guys illegally trapping. There were several of the same traps that Dolly had gotten caught in. A dozen beaver pelts lay in a corner with some other pelts from other animals. They had a map with each trap location marked, including the one they had found in the pasture where Dolly had gotten hurt. Beau and Adam just looked at each other and shook their heads.

The sheriff spoke up. "Gentlemen, we're going to need you to come into town with us."

Buzz Cut looked at the sheriff and kicked Greasy Hair. "I told you we shouldn't have brought the weed. The cops are here."

Greasy Hair said, "Hullo officer. We've only got the legal limit. Not too much and we ain't driving, so we're good."

Sheriff Carlson recited the Revised Miranda and asked the men if they understood their rights.

"Yep, heard 'em before," Buzz Cut said.

Greasy Hair nodded. "I understand, but we ain't got too much pot, I tell you."

Drake Carlson shook his head. "We're not here for marijuana. You are trespassing on private land. And you've been trapping with illegal traps on the same private land, without permission. So, I need you to come with me."

"Well, hell. The jig is up I suppose." Greasy Hair tried to stand and was unsuccessful, falling back down and laughing like a loon. "Can't help you, officer."

"We're going to have to carry these idiots, aren't we?" Drew said.

Buzz Cut said, "Hey, we're not idiots—just a little high. Been celebrating a bit with the first set of skins we sold at a primo price to some furriers."

Beau shook his head and looked at his brothers. He could see disgust written on both their faces. "Give me the keys, Drew. I'll bring the SUV in closer so we can get it loaded with all the evidence and the idiots."

Beau took the keys and walked out into the fresh sweet air. It was going to take some airing to get all the weed smell out of the cabin. They might need to fumigate, and they would definitely need to wash—or maybe burn—all the bedding and towels. But at least no more cattle would get caught in the traps. They would go out and collect all the ones carefully marked on the map. At least the guys were thorough and they wouldn't be stumbling upon traps for years.

Beau sent a family text.

> Beau: Poachers found. No trouble encountered.
> Problem solved. Will share, maybe an hour.

He got a flurry of thumbs up and happy face texts back.

ALYSSA WAS glad to hear they had the trappers in custody, she hoped that meant no other animals would be hurt or killed. She wanted to avoid Beau, but she knew her curiosity was too strong to not go find out what happened. So, she shut down the tablet and plugged it in to recharge, and left her room to join the family that would be assembling to hear the news.

She met Emma in the hall. "I'm so glad they caught them, aren't you, Alyssa? I think we should make popcorn and hot chocolate while we wait for Beau and Adam to get back to tell us the news. We can pretend we're at the movie. Beau and Adam are both great story tellers, and since Beau didn't say much in the text, there is a story to be told. I can guarantee that."

"How did you get that out of the text?"

"Whenever he says he'll *share* that means there's a story involved."

Alyssa nodded. "Good to know."

"So, let's get some popcorn popping and some homemade hot chocolate started."

"Homemade hot chocolate? Like from milk and real chocolate?"

"Absolutely. None of that powdered stuff in our family." Emma wrinkled her nose like she'd just stepped in cow manure.

Alyssa smiled. "We only have real hot chocolate made from scratch on Christmas morning. The rest of the time, it's powdered."

"Oh, you poor thing. We will take care of that today."

When they got to the kitchen, Meg was already in there bustling around. "I figured hot chocolate and popcorn was in order."

Emma nodded. "Yep, I was thinking that too. Poor Alyssa here only gets real hot chocolate on Christmas morning, the rest of the time, they have powdered."

Meg had the exact same expression she'd seen on Emma's face. "Oh, you poor dear."

Alyssa smiled. "We just save it for special occasions, is all."

Meg laughed. "You've never been treated to the Adam and Beau Show before. I wish Drew could be here, too. The three of them is even better. The twins said everything was quiet in the pasture, so they are coming in and leaving it to the hired hands. No one wants to miss Beau and Adam *sharing*."

Alyssa was getting curious about what this sharing entailed.

Meg's cell phone buzzed. "It's a text from Drew and he

said to get some sandwiches ready for Adam and Beau, because they are going to be hungry. That's odd, but I trust his judgement, so let's make some sandwiches and get a few heartier items together. Chase and Cade might be hungry, too."

They all three bustled around the kitchen preparing a feast.

CHAPTER 16

*C*hase and Cade arrived first. Chase hollered as he dashed past, "Don't let them start without us."

Alyssa startled as the guys flew through the kitchen. "What?"

Emma said, "They'll clean up a bit from being out weighing and tagging the new calves."

Alyssa nodded. "Right. That makes sense. But is it really that urgent that they don't miss anything?"

Emma laughed. "You'll have to be the judge of that, after you see the *show*."

The twins were back in record time washed up, with clean sweats on. Cade looked around the kitchen where everyone had gathered at the table with a feast in the middle. "They're not here yet?"

Chase frowned, "They should be here by now. They should have been ahead of us. I hope nothing went wrong."

Just then, a truck pulled into the driveway and there was a lot of laughing and door slamming. Meg lifted an eyebrow and looked at Travis, who just shrugged.

Adam and Beau rounded the corner from the mudroom giggling like a couple of school girls.

Adam spotted the food. "Score! I'm fricken starving."

Both grabbed a sandwich and inhaled it before they even sat down at the table. Alyssa noticed a slight whiff of something. It smelled like pot.

Chase sniffed and shook his head. "They're stoned."

Beau nodded. "Most probably. Those poachers were having themselves quite the clam bake in cabin three."

Adam grinned and spoke around the food in his mouth. "Yeah, we left the windows open to air it out some, but I think we might need to fumigate."

Nodding his head, Beau said, "And burn the bedding and towels."

Adam shrugged and then grabbed another sandwich to devour.

Travis asked, "So they were not only poaching on our land, but they had made themselves at home in cabin three? And were smoking pot in there heavy enough to give you two a contact high?"

Adam grinned and Beau nodded. "I imagine all eight of us have a contact high. You could hardly see in there, it was filled with so much smoke. By the time we carried them and all the evidence out of the cabin and got it into Drew's patrol rig, we were all feeling a little woozy. I think every animal within a mile radius is going to be high. Adam here drove five miles an hour to get back home without running his truck into a tree."

Grandpa K asked, "So, you're sure it was them?"

Adam giggled. "Oh, yeah. There was evidence everywhere. Traps, skins, and a very helpful map detailing where all the traps are set. It shouldn't take us long to go get them tomorrow. I took pictures of the map with my phone."

"Those guys were so stoned they happily told us that they had used some of their first fur sales to purchase the weed. But Greasy Hair wanted to make sure we knew they had no more weed than the legal limit. Buzz Cut was certain we arrested them for the pot. We tried to explain it was for the illegal trapping, but I'm not sure it registered. Greasy Hair couldn't even stand on his own he was so toasted." Beau reported.

"Buzz Cut and Greasy Hair? Didn't they have real names?" Alyssa asked.

Beau grinned at her in a sappy way. "I'm sure they did sweet darlin', but I was calling them those names before I was told the real ones, and they are easier to remember." Beau slowly turned his sappy grin toward his mother and asked if there were any cookies.

Alyssa felt her face grow warm and hoped no one else noticed Beau's slip up. She busied herself stirring her hot chocolate, hoping everyone would assume her pink cheeks were from the steam. She looked up. Adam was looking at her intently, despite his dilated pupils and stoned expression.

Emma got up to get some cookies for Beau. "Now start at the beginning and tell us the whole story. How did Drew know where to look?"

They started in telling the tale from start to finish and Alyssa had to admit it was quite funny. They tag teamed each other in the telling and both perspectives were highly amusing. When they were finally done all the food was eaten— including the whole package of cookies. It was nearly midnight when the party broke up, and they all headed to their rooms for some much-needed sleep. Adam and Beau were both dragging once they came down from their high.

Beau reached out to her as they split off toward their rooms. He touched his fingertips to hers and said quietly, "We'll talk tomorrow."

She nodded and went into her room. She wasn't quite

sure what she wanted to say to him, but she was certain the kiss and what he'd said after needed to be discussed. If only to clear the air and be on the same page going forward. But she wasn't looking forward to it.

~

BEAU STAGGERED TO HIS ROOM, he was so exhausted. He wasn't a fan of marijuana. He'd tried it once in high school and felt the same as he did now, too tired to even move. And he couldn't get his brain to think at all. He was so full, from inhaling all that food, he thought he might explode. He couldn't figure out why people liked pot, in his opinion it only made people exhausted, fat and stupid. But no one asked his opinion, so to each his own.

He wished he could talk with Alyssa tonight, he would rather not wait until tomorrow, but he didn't have the ability. He was certain he wouldn't even be able to remember what he wanted to say, much less string two words together to say it. Nope, it was going to have to wait.

He dragged his clothes off as he stumbled toward his bed. He'd pick them up tomorrow, right now he needed sleep. He fell face first into his bed with just his skivvies on and barely managed to pull the covers over himself before he was asleep.

CHAPTER 17

*B*eau woke a few hours later to the chirp of his phone running out of power. *Dammit I didn't plug it in.* He dragged himself out of bed and across the room to where he'd dropped his jeans. Good thing he'd turned the volume back up to high after the poacher hunting, otherwise he might not have heard it beep and wouldn't have a cell all day. Hard to handle emergencies when no one could contact him. He could always hang with Alyssa and get texts with her. A fun idea, but not really practical to have the two medically trained people in one place.

He plugged the damn phone in to charge and crawled back in bed, but now he was awake and thinking about Alyssa—and what he wanted to tell her. He didn't know what to say because he was totally fascinated by the woman. He wanted to bury himself deep inside her for about a year or two and take her every way he could possibly dream up. But the fact of the matter was, they had separate lives in different states. So, they had no future beyond this season, and the season was a damn busy one, so they didn't really have time for a romance—or even a roll in the hay, because he was certain one time would never be enough. No, it was probably best to forget his infatuation with her, but it might just be the hardest thing he'd ever had to do. Like cutting off a limb. The attraction he felt for her was off the charts of any previous relationship he'd ever had. What a damn mess, but it was probably best to resist her.

With that crappy decision, he managed to drift off to sleep again. But this time his dreams were all about what his life could be like if he let himself be with Alyssa. And those dreams were hot. So hot, that when his alarm went off he wanted to smash it to bits, and go back to sleep so he could enjoy Alyssa in ways he never could in reality.

But real life was calling, and it took precedence. Sometimes he wished he had a looser work ethic, but he didn't. He needed to get his ass out of bed and in the shower. He was going to have a full day working the ranch, and talking to Alyssa, and who knew what else. Adam had mentioned last night that he and some of the hands would go out and collect the traps, so that was one thing he didn't have to worry about.

There was a knock on his door, so he went to answer it. Speak of the devil. Adam was standing at his door. He pushed in and didn't even seem to notice Beau wasn't dressed. Adam paced the room and ran his hands through his hair making it stick up funny.

He stopped and turned. "I probably shouldn't say anything. You're both adults, but what in the hell are you thinking? She's nearly a decade younger than you. You're supposed to be mentoring her, not hitting on her. Dammit, Beau."

Beau had no idea where Adam had gotten his information so he didn't know what to say. "What are you talking about?"

"Last night, you looking at her like a lovesick puppy and

calling her sweet darling. I hope to hell no one else noticed you acting like a dumb ass."

"I did? Are you sure? We were both pretty lit."

"Alyssa turned bright red." Adam frowned and folded his arms.

"Fuck."

"Are you sleeping with her?"

Beau's head snapped up. "What? No. We kissed. Once. I'm going to talk to her today."

"It better be to break it off, because you have no business hitting on that child."

Now he was pissed. "She's not a child. She's twenty-two and I'll hit on her if I want. Mind your own damn business, Adam. I know what I'm doing."

"Do you? You're seven years older than she is. She's a cutie, I don't deny it, but—well, I hope to hell you do know what you're doing. I'm not sure I believe it."

"Thanks for the vote of confidence, big brother."

"Shit, I'm going out to round up those traps. Try not to be a dumb ass."

Adam stormed out of Beau's room and slammed the door. That went well. Not.

ALYSSA WAS in the kitchen having a nice hot cup of coffee when Adam stormed through the door. He stopped and looked at her, then shook his head and continued out of the room. Grandpa K, was still in the kitchen from getting a late start due to the activities last night, was having his bowl of Rice Krispies. Alyssa had decided it was his breakfast dessert, because he had bacon and eggs or biscuits and gravy or something more substantial and then finished up with his favorite cereal, every day.

Grandpa K looked at her and raised an eyebrow. "What's up with him?"

"I have no idea."

"Maybe it's just a hangover."

"Maybe." But she wondered if there was more to it. He might have noticed Beau acting different toward her last night—when he was high and not under strict control.

"I better get a move on. Daylight's burning. Have a good day, little girl."

Alyssa kissed his cheek. "You too, Grandpa K."

She wondered if her day would be good or bad. She hadn't been able to sleep much last night, wondering what Beau was going to say when he was sober. She got a bagel and popped it into the toaster—she didn't know if her stomach could handle anything heavier than that. She'd always tended to carry her stress in her stomach. But going out for a full day's work on just coffee wasn't a good idea, either. She could also carry a granola bar for later. That was a good plan—then, if she threw up after talking to Beau she would have some sustenance to carry her over to lunch. Okay, enough of the melodrama. It wasn't like she was in love with the man or anything. Yes, she respected him and yes, she thought he was hot and yes, he made her toes curl when he kissed her. But love? Nope, not her. Dear God, she hoped not anyway.

CHAPTER 18

*B*eau buttoned his jeans and pulled on his shirt when his cell chimed with a text.

> *Travis: Trouble in the birthing barn.*
> *Alyssa: Coming*
> *Beau: Me too.*

Beau rushed out of his room buttoning his shirt as he went. His father was one of the most capable ranchers he knew, so if he was calling for help it was serious. Alyssa was in the mud room with her boots and coat on, grabbing up first aid supplies when he flew in the door.

"Go, I'm right behind you."

She nodded and ran outside while he stuffed his feet into his boots, yanked his coat off the rack and hustled out right after her.

They hit the barn at the same time, he grabbed some of the supplies to lighten her load.

His dad called out, "I've got a nearly dead calf."

From the other end of the barn, Grandpa K hollered, "I've got twins."

Beau grimaced and looked at Alyssa. "Want the twins?"

She nodded and seemed relieved. "I'll yell if I need you."

"You do that." And then he hustled to one end of the barn and she hurried to the other end.

Travis said, "It's not looking good, son. He's not responding. I got here just as she dropped him and he couldn't stand. I pulled her into another stall to give you room."

"Let's see what we can do." Beau went to work on the little guy.

~

ALYSSA RUSHED into the stall where Grandpa K was.

"One dropped just fine but the other one is having trouble. I can't tell if he's breech or wrapped up in the cord."

Alyssa put on some gloves and examined the situation. "Looks like he's wrapped in the cord. I think I can get him unstuck."

A few minutes later she had the little guy freed and a couple more pushes from the mother and the calf slid out. It was a little underweight, but nothing that would keep her from thriving. But then the real trouble began—the mother refused the second calf. She'd bonded with the first one—a male—and she wanted nothing to do with the smaller female.

Alyssa tried to get the dam to accept the girl, but she wasn't having it. She didn't know what to do. Her heart was pounding and her mind was frantically flipping through the ways to get a mother to accept her baby. She'd tried every one of them.

Alyssa hollered, "Beau she's rejecting the second one. I've tried everything I know to do and she's pushing her away."

Beau came into the stall. "Mine didn't make it. Let's try

grafting this little heifer to the dam that lost hers. If she won't take her, we can always bottle feed her, I suppose That's a hell of a lot of work, but we could manage it."

"Yeah, but let's see if we can get the other mother to accept this one. Great idea."

Beau took the little one into the mother and gave the dam a minute to see if she would accept or reject her—he'd done his best to make her think it was her own calf. She acted a little uncertain at first, but then accepted her and started cleaning her and allowed her to nurse.

All four of them breathed a sigh of relief.

Travis said, "I'll take care of the one that didn't make it.'

Beau nodded. "Thanks, Dad."

Alyssa and Beau washed up, then gathered up the medical supplies and their jackets they'd tossed aside and walked out of the barn. Beau looked over at her and she was sure he could see the tears in her eyes and how fragile she was feeling. He took her hand and led her off to the side of the barn to where there was a small bench and guided her to sit. Then he crouched in front of her and took her hands.

"You did good in there."

"Oh, Beau, I was so scared. When the calf was stuck I wasn't sure I could get it loose. But I sucked it up and got her free. I was so relieved, but then the mother rejected her, and I didn't know what to do. That dam just had no interest in her little girl calf. She had her boy, and she wasn't interested in another one. I know it's mean, but I was almost relieved when you said yours hadn't made it."

He shook his head and rubbed her knuckles. "That wasn't mean, Alyssa. I was worried about how that mother was going to react when she didn't have a calf. I was almost relieved when you had one that was rejected. I was worried she might not accept it, but she did."

She sighed, feeling like the world rested on her shoulders. "It's been a crazy couple of days."

"It has. It always seems to go in waves like that. Weeks of normal, everyday, easy births and then, wham, a week of craziness. But I've been relieved to have you at my side."

"Even when I practically forced you to kiss me?" she asked him shyly.

Beau laughed. "That's been the best part of both days combined. I enjoyed kissing you and would like to do a lot more of it...."

Alyssa put her hand over his mouth. "Let's just leave it right there. I don't have any strength left to talk about it anymore than that right now. So, I want to leave it at you would like to do a lot more of it."

Beau smiled under her hand. When she lifted it he said, "Fine by me."

"Good." She leaned in and gave him a quick kiss.

He groaned and pulled her in for another longer one, and she reveled in the action. She loved the warmth and the gentleness and wanted to stay like that all day, kissing the man, but they needed to get busy with their jobs and he hadn't eaten yet.

She pulled back. "We have work to do, cowboy. And you need to eat first."

"Your lips are all the sustenance I need." But then his stomach growled, contradicting his words.

She laughed and stood up from the bench. "Yeah, well, your stomach doesn't agree. Let's move it."

He muttered all the way to the house about how his stomach was not the one in charge and it needed to quit being so bossy. Alyssa just laughed and decided to take it as a compliment, that he wanted to kiss her more than eat.

CHAPTER 19

*B*eau knew he shouldn't leave the discussion for later, but he did not push the subject, because he liked kissing her. Once they had *the talk* there would be no more kissing. So, he could grant her wish and put it off for a while. Truth be told, he was enjoying this interlude of attraction a lot. If there were any way they could make it work, that would be amazing. It never could, but for right now—today—he would let it ride. Plenty of time left to get on the right track. For now, a little meandering felt too good.

He followed her into the house and wanted to start singing. Maybe he could get his old guitar down and write a couple verses of a song. He hadn't done anything like that in years, but for some reason it seemed like a good idea to him. They hit the kitchen and he loaded up on breakfast. She took a few nibbles of food as she sat with him.

"Aren't you going to eat more than that?"

She smiled at him and his whole body went on alert. "I had a bagel earlier and I have a granola bar for later, so this is plenty. Wouldn't want to get fat."

He looked at her body and saw no hint of that happening any time soon. "No worries there darlin'; you are beautiful."

She flushed a delightful shade of pink. "Now, stop that."

"Stop what? Looking at you? Noticing you're beautiful? Or saying it out loud instead of just thinking it?"

"I don't know, all of it. Do you really think I'm beautiful?"

He shrugged and pointed at her with his fork. "Of course. Do you not have a mirror? I thought you were beautiful the first moment I saw you all dressed up in your city slicker duds."

She frowned at him. "No, you didn't. You were so mean to me."

He rubbed a hand across the back of his neck. Time to come clean. "I was jealous."

"Of whom exactly? You were mean before I ever set eyes on anyone else."

"I thought you'd come for a riding lesson—that you were Drake Carlson's new girlfriend."

"The sheriff? He's older than my father! That's ridiculous. Did you think I was some kind of gold digger or trophy girlfriend?"

Beau could feel his face heating and looked down at his breakfast.

"You did. Well, I don't know whether to be amused or pissed off that you would think that about me."

"I didn't know anything about you. I was supposed to be giving a riding lesson to Drake's new girlfriend, and you drove in. What was I supposed to think?"

"Maybe you were supposed to listen to my name and think I was the intern. I even said I was the intern." She wagged her finger at him.

"I didn't hear anything. I was so caught up in anger and desire I couldn't concentrate."

That stopped her in her tracks. "Desire? For me?"

"Well, yes. Who the hell else would I have been lusting over? You took one step out of that car and I was gone."

She sat back and a slow smile slid across her face. "Hmm, I think I like that. At least it tells me why you were such a dick the first few hours I was here. I couldn't figure out how you could go from being so mean to such a good guy."

"Yeah, I am sorry about all that, but it didn't take you too long to put me in my place."

Alyssa laughed and the sound slid through him, igniting every nerve ending. "That was a convenient turn in the conversation. I just took advantage of it to let you know that even at eight years old, I knew better than to wear my city slicker duds to a working ranch."

He got up and put their plates in the sink, then he tugged on her hand and pulled her up to stand next to him. He slowly backed her up against the counter as he covered his mouth with hers. His hands were on her hips and drawing her in as his mouth played with hers. She put her hands in his hair and clutched. He might end up bald, but he had no intention of stopping her.

They fit together like puzzle pieces, his hardness to her softness. She wriggled, getting closer, and he lifted her up for an even better fit. She sighed, and he was gone. He could spend a week supping from her sweet lips, her soft body wrapped in his. He was lost in a haze of longing and sensuality.

"I guess that seals the bet. Neither one of us get her—big brother does," Chase said.

"Damn, too slow, too late for us," Cade answered.

Beau pulled back from heaven and turned his head toward his two grinning brothers. He looked back at Alyssa as she slowly opened her eyes and blinked. Then she lowered her forehead to his chest and whispered, "Are they gone yet?"

He looked back at his idiot brothers. "Nope, still there."

"Hey, we came for breakfast. Not our fault you're making out in the kitchen," Cade whined.

Alyssa sighed. "I guess they do have a point, and we *are* supposed to be out checking on the herd."

"I suppose, if you're going to get all practical." Beau teased. He put her down and took her hand and without even acknowledging his brothers, they walked out the door to get to work.

～

ALYSSA FOLLOWED BEAU, but just before they cleared the door she turned back to the twins who were watching them leave, and gave them a wink and sly grin. Delight lit their faces and they both gave her two thumbs up.

Her heart was as light as air—like champagne was running through her veins. Maybe this was only temporary, but she was going to enjoy it while she could. She was long overdue a nice guy and a few kisses. She'd been working so hard at her degree, she'd pushed relationships to the far bottom of the list of things to do. There had been a couple of guys that had asked her out, but she had let them know, up front, she wasn't interested in dating. Study partners? Maybe. Friends to eat with? Sure. Guys to date? Nope, not going there. But she wasn't studying every second now and wasn't trying to memorize tons of information and pass tests and write papers, so she had time to indulge—at least a little.

Beau asked, "Pasture or barn?"

Alyssa looked at the bright blue sky and decided she wanted to enjoy the pretty morning. "Pasture. We can trade off after lunch."

"Sounds good to me. I'll see you later."

"Beau?" He turned back, and she went up on her tiptoes to give him a soft warm kiss. "Think of me?"

"Hell, I'm going to have to fight to think of anything else."

She got in the truck and headed out to the pasture. A couple of the hired hands were out there keeping an eye on things. She would be joining them for any medical issues that came up. Roving to look for issues. When she got out to the pasture, she found the two guys working to weigh and tag several calves that looked like they'd all been born at the same time. She rolled down her window. "Need some help?"

Cliff yelled back, "No, we're good, but we haven't made it out to the far corner yet because we've been busy here— would you mind?"

"Happy to. Holler if you need me."

"Will do."

Alyssa waved and drove off in the direction they had pointed. It was such a beautiful day. A little chilly, but not extreme for this time of year. When she got out to the farthest corner she was glad she'd come out. There were two heifers that had wandered off from the herd and both seemed to be giving birth at the same time. They didn't appear to be having any trouble, so she just sat back and watched carefully as the cows labored. One finished giving birth so she weighed and tagged the calf. Then noticed the second dam was having a bit more difficulty, so she thought maybe she should see if she could help the process along.

She could do a little manual pulling—nothing too inva-sive, just help the little guy come out quicker. She checked to make sure the calf wasn't caught up in the cord. That didn't seem to be the case. It looked like the mother was kind of small. She checked the tag to see which heifer this was and thought back to the birthing records she'd been studying. She remembered they had used a bull that produced a bit larger calves and realized this dam had gone a little longer than she should have—just a few days, but that could make a difference in calf size. So, maybe the calf was a little too large. She thought about calling Beau, but decided she could handle it alone.

She hunkered down to help pull gently on the calf to help it come out easier. It looked like that was going to work, so every time the mother had a contraction she pulled gently on the calf. It took some time, but the little guy was finally born. She weighed it and realized it was a little larger than was optimum, for this breed of heifer to birth without assistance. She would need to tell Beau about it.

She finally got ready to leave and realized a storm front had come in while she was focused on the birth, and there was light snow falling. She pulled out her phone to check the time and noticed it was later than she thought. She decided to text Beau to let him know where she was, and that she would be heading in when the mother she'd been helping head butted her. Her phone flew out of her hands and landed with a crash, face down on a rock. Dammit, she hoped it wasn't broken, but it was. The screen was shattered and the whole thing had shut down and wasn't turning back on.

She climbed in the truck to head back to the ranch and realized she didn't have her GPS to guide her, and the spring storm was not going to help. In the few minutes it took to break her phone, the storm had dropped down and it was snowing hard. Visibility was nearly non-existent and she couldn't see any familiar landmarks. *Well hell, now what?* She didn't want to just sit there and wait—no one knew exactly where she was. The hired hands would have a general idea— if they even noticed she had not returned. But should she be driving in near-blizzard conditions? How long would a spring snow storm last in the Colorado mountains? She laughed a little hysterically thinking she could Google it if her phone hadn't been destroyed. The truck had plenty of gas, so she could just wait it out—providing it was only a couple of hours. Better than driving into a ditch or a beaver dam or the flippin' river. She decided to stay right where she was, at least for now.

CHAPTER 20

*B*eau was starting to get concerned. Alyssa should have been back over an hour ago and a damn spring storm had just blown in and it was snowing like hell. He'd sent her a couple of texts but got no response. If she was busy with one of the cattle that would make sense; she wouldn't stop to answer a text. He tried to call, but it went straight to voice mail—not a good sign. Maybe she was on the phone and would call him back.

His Spidey sense was tingling though, so he didn't want to wait. She wasn't from Colorado and she'd said they didn't get much snow in the Chelan area due to the lake keeping the area warmer. In the mountains of Colorado, a spring storm like this could dump a couple of feet of snow. It could kill visibility and hide dangerous objects like rocks and downed trees.

He decided to go out to the bunk house to see if one of the hands that had been out at the same time had any information. It wasn't easy to even get that far with the blowing snow. When he entered the building, his brothers and several of the ranch hands were having a rousing poker game. Other than checking out the birthing barn, there wasn't much they could do in the whiteout conditions. The cattle in the pasture were on their own for an hour or two.

Beau cleared his throat. "So, Alyssa isn't back yet for our switch up. Anyone know where she might be?"

Cliff said, "She was going up to check the far corner of the pasture. Bud and I were busy with a half-dozen calves that came at the same damn time and hadn't made it that far. When we got done, we just assumed she'd be back and didn't drive up to check. We brought a new calf and its mother in for you to be able to keep an eye on—the little one was kind of weak."

Beau frowned and bit back his temper. "So, she went up there alone?"

Cliff looked out the window at the storm raging. "Yeah, she did. Pretty rough out there, huh? We didn't know we were going to have one of these freak storms. The sun was shining and there wasn't a cloud, when she came out."

Beau slapped his hat on his leg. He couldn't take his frustration out on the men. No one could have predicted this storm blowing in like it did. The forecast had said there might be some weather tomorrow, but nothing today. But that was Colorado weather in the high country—unpredictable as hell. "I know, damn storm snuck up on us. But we might have to go out and find her when this lets up. She's not answering her cell."

"Did you try the truck two-way radio? We don't use them much these days, but they still should work, and it comes on automatically. She has to be in the truck—let's hope she's not out in this."

"Good idea." Beau was out the door and to the closest truck in seconds. Before he even got it started the twins got in with him.

"Just checking on our girl," Cade said.

Beau nodded and reached down to where the radio snugly fit under the dashboard. He grabbed the mic, selected the frequency for the vet truck, and keyed the mic. "Alyssa, this is Beau. Can you hear me?"

Not a sound.

Chase said tightly, "Just keep saying it every few minutes."

Beau nodded and tried again.

∽

ALYSSA WAS FLIPPIN' freezing. She was trying not to run the truck's heater too often in case this damn storm lasted hours. She would rather be cold in the daylight, than cold in the dark. She'd used the warming blankets stored in the truck to make a tent for the two mothers and babies. Yeah, they were animals and should be fine, but she wasn't going to let them freeze on her watch—at least not until it was a them-or-her type of situation.

It was time to start the truck to heat the cab; she was getting too cold. As she cranked the starter she thought she heard something. She looked out the windows but there was nothing except white. Hopefully she wasn't going crazy. The engine roared to life and a few seconds later blissful warmth came out the vents. She sighed in relief and again there was an unfamiliar noise. It sounded like a very faint voice. She rolled down the window to listen and got a face full of snow and nothing else. It wasn't the radio—she'd turned that off earlier, when the forecast didn't give any pertinent information about the weather and how long it was going to last. They were laughing it off and telling everyone welcome to springtime in Colorado. Dumbasses.

She sat quiet, barely breathing, until she heard it again. It sounded like her name coming from the floor. She leaned down to hear better and spied a two-way radio tucked up under the dash. She cranked the volume up and grabbed the mic just as Beau bellowed. "Alyssa, this is Beau, can you hear me?"

She didn't know whether to cheer or cry, so she clicked the mic and said in a shuddery voice, "Yes, Beau. I can hear you."

"Well, thank God. It's about fucking time you answered. I was about to have a heart attack."

"Yes, I'm fine. Thank you for asking so sweetly. And the calves and their mothers are doing well, also."

Beau laughed and then groaned. "Are you really fine? Where are you? What happened? Why didn't you answer your phone?"

"I will be happy to answer all your questions as soon as you tell me how long this damn blizzard is going to last." Her voice got shriller with each word. And before Beau could answer, the snow stopped and the sun came out. *Well, fuck.*

"About now. Looks finished to me."

Alyssa sighed. "You have the craziest weather I have ever seen."

"Yep, I'll come get you now, so you don't have to drive in the white stuff and the mud that will be soon to follow. If you tell me where you are."

"But I'll still have to drive this one back."

"No, the twins are with me. We'll come get you and they can drive this truck back. What coordinates are you at?"

She was feeling so relieved that she had tears threatening and she could hardly speak. She hiccupped. "My phone got smashed on a rock, so I don't know the coordinates. But I'm in the far corner by that tree that's all twisted up."

"Perfect. We'll be there soon. How about you stay on the radio and tell us what happened? I'll give the mic to Chase, so Cade doesn't talk your ear off."

"Okay, hurry Beau. I've had enough alone time today." She started telling them the story, and before she was finished she saw a truck coming toward her. Tears of relief welled in her eyes and her throat closed. She didn't realize she was quite as frightened as she was, until there was nothing left to fear. She let the mic drop to the seat beside her and leaned her head on the steering wheel and let the tears come.

Beau opened her door and pulled her into his arms and held her until the waterworks stopped. Chase gathered up the warming blankets, while Cade checked the cattle to find them happy and dry.

Beau chuckled. "You used the warming blankets on the cattle instead of keeping yourself warm? You do realize they are animals and used to being outside."

"Not the calves—they weren't even dry when this snow started. I wasn't going to let all my hard work freeze when I could sit in the truck and stay warm."

Beau touched her hands. "You feel kind of cold to me."

"I didn't know how long this snow would last and I didn't want to run out of gas if it got dark."

Beau's jaw tightened. "There is no way in hell I would have left you out here until dark. I'd have gotten the snow-mobiles out, and come after you long before the sun set. Plus, spring storms like that one only last a couple of hours at most, providing the sun is shining before it happens. If we'd been socked in with clouds that would have been a different story."

"Good to know, now. But I didn't know then and my phone was smashed, so I couldn't even Google it." Her throat closed again and tears threatened.

Beau looked at her. "Let's get you back to the house. You must be starving."

"I had my granola bar from this morning."

Beau kissed her forehead. "Scoot over and we can get out of here before all this snow melts and turns to mud."

"It won't melt that fast, will it?"

"Wait and see."

She was surprised when much of the snow was melted by the time they got back to the house. Once the storm had passed through it had brought sunshine and warmer temperatures. *Colorado has very odd weather.*

CHAPTER 21

*B*eau was just barely holding it together. He'd been scared shitless when he couldn't get ahold of her, and the damn snow was coming down so hard. He'd lightened the facts up a bit because she was distraught, but people had died in freak spring storms like that one. Being out in the warm spring day and not prepared for blizzard like conditions, it could get ugly quick. It was true that normally the snow didn't last too long, but it didn't take much time in the high altitude to get hypothermia and frostbite, or to get lost and disoriented, or fall into the river, or beaver dams, or down a cliff, or break a leg in a gopher hole.

He was making himself crazy, thinking of all the bad things that *could* have happened. They hadn't because Alyssa was smart enough to stay put and ride out the storm. Using the gas sparingly was even a smart move. Covering the cattle with the warming blankets instead of using them herself? Not such a smart move, but if truth be told he might have done the same thing. At least for a while, until the calves were warm and dry. But he wished she'd used them on herself—he didn't like the idea of her being cold and alone.

The protocol was that the rovers were supposed to go with the vet to check the herd; none of them were supposed to be alone. They did get separated once in a while, but it wasn't a good idea. And it sure as hell wasn't going to happen to Alyssa again, if he had anything to say about it.

"You're not going to get all crazy about this, are you?"

Shit, could she read his mind? "What makes you say that?"

"You're not talking to me, you're practically steaming, and you're so tense you can barely drive. I appreciate the sentiment, but I didn't do anything foolish and I am just fine."

He forced himself to relax and took her hand in his. "You did everything exactly right—well, except maybe giving the blankets to the cattle."

"Like you wouldn't have done the same."

He laughed. "Maybe, but not if push came to shove. If it was me or the cattle, I would vote for me."

"Oh, don't you worry your pretty little head about that. If it started to get dark I had every intention of taking the blankets back. Survival of the fittest and all that."

"Good to know."

Alyssa said, "So, about that calf being too big."

"Yeah, we're going to have to look into what happened there. If she was really a few days late as you think she was, then we missed something somewhere. I'll have to look at the printouts we send with the hands that have the list of which cattle to keep an eye on, and see how the ball got dropped. Another day or two with no one around and we might have lost the heifer."

"My thoughts exactly, but even if one of the hands dropped the ball, it's ultimately our responsibility to check and make sure nothing gets through the cracks."

"I can't imagine either of us missing it, let alone both of us, so we'll need to check the database to see what happened."

"You can do that while I eat. I'm starving. A granola bar

doesn't last too long, and pulling that calf out wasn't the easiest thing I've done." Her stomach rumbled to emphasize the point.

"Perfect, I'll make you a plate of food while you change out of those cold, dirty clothes and into something warm and dry." Her hands had been like ice out there and he wanted to make sure she was on her way to warming up. Hypothermia was not fun.

They got back to the house and once Alyssa had a plate of food in front of her that would feed a small army, he brought up the database and checked the birth records for this year. "Just as I thought, that heifer is showing a calf born last week. I'll run a search and see what dams haven't given birth that would be due this week and might have a similar number. It might be a number swapping kind of error."

"Easy to do, but kind of scary to let happen. Have you had this type of issue in the past?"

"Unfortunately, yes. One of the hired hands, Lloyd, has dyslexia and has been known to swap numbers. It's never caused anything other than some confusion and running around to determine the right numbering. And he's supposed to have the other guy he's out with check the tags to make sure they match."

She frowned. "We had that flurry of births last week, like today, where there were so many at the same time, that they might have separated like we had happen today."

"Yeah, we might need to hire a few more people to get the buddy system better reinforced. I found three that have similar numbers. Two of which gave birth last week and one that Lloyd was the tagger. I'm betting that's the one. Same breed, same birth year, one is 189 the other is 198."

Alyssa nodded. "Sounds like you found it."

"Now we have to verify it, fix the tags and the database, and have a chat with Lloyd and his assigned buddy." He got out his phone and sent a text to Lloyd and Kent telling them to check in with him before their next shift.

∼

ALYSSA WAS glad they had figured out what had caused the problem, and she was glad it hadn't been her fault. She'd been a little concerned that maybe she'd been daydreaming about Beau one day and had mis-tagged a calf.

She didn't want someone else to be in trouble, but if they made a mistake they needed to be more careful. That mother could have died from the calf being too large for her to push out alone. Especially if that spring blizzard had started any earlier and no one would have been there.

She was just finishing up the last of her lunch, surprised she'd managed to pack it all away, when Lloyd and Kent knocked on the mud room door. Beau answered the door and ushered the men into the kitchen, which she thought was a little odd and wondered if she should excuse herself to give them privacy.

He left the men standing and sat back down at the table. "So, Alyssa here got caught out in that blizzard this afternoon. Want to guess why?"

Kent shook his head. "No, sir. But I'm guessing it had something to do with me and Lloyd."

Beau folded his arms. "Damn good guess, Kent. Lloyd, do you want to hazard a guess?"

Lloyd looked down at the floor. "I'm guessing I screwed something up again. I'm sorry boss—and you too, Alyssa."

Beau said firmly. "Now Lloyd, we all know you have trouble with getting your numbers mixed, and that's nothing to be ashamed of, and nothing I am going to be angry about. However, it's been our policy to have Kent verify your tags.

118

Can either of you recall a time recently when that didn't happen?"

Lloyd nodded. "I have an idea when it might have happened, but it wasn't on purpose."

"If I thought it was on purpose, you'd already be collecting your last paycheck. Both of you. Tell me what happened."

Lloyd looked down at the floor then he looked up and squared his shoulders. "Last Wednesday when we went out to patrol the herd, we were coming up on the last quadrant, when we ran into a group of heifers that all decided to give birth at the same damn time. Oh, excuse me Alyssa, the same darn time. So, Kent and me split up. I took half, and he took half. We were just finishing up and Kent was checking my half, when one of those drones flew overhead. Only it was too damn, um, darn low and it startled all of us. The cattle scattered seeking shelter or trying to get away from the darn thing. Kent and I looked around to see if we could find anyone in control of the robot, but couldn't see anyone. The drone finally took off, but by then the cattle who'd given birth were scattered and Kent and I had both lost count as to how many of mine he'd checked. We thought maybe he'd been done, but I'm guessing that maybe we were wrong about that."

Kent nodded. "Yes sir, we really thought we'd gotten them all done, but that drone scared the bejeezes out of all of us."

Beau had unfolded his arms and nodded at the men. "I can understand the problem and most of it wasn't your fault. But there are a couple of things I want you to do differently if it ever happens again. First, if you see a drone over our land I want you to let one of the family members know about it asap. We need to check it out. Best way to handle it is to send the family a group text with the coordinates of where you are, and the direction the thing is heading. Second, when you turn in your reports at shift end, write up what happened and let us know that we might need to verify tag numbers on your group from that day."

"Yes, sir," both men said in tandem.

Beau then told the guys what had happened today with the late heifer and asked Alyssa to elaborate where needed. He wasn't unkind, but he wanted them to know the cause and effect of their actions. When the story was finished, both of them apologized to Beau and Alyssa again and said they would do better, if it happened some other time. Beau shook hands with the men and dismissed them to get back to work.

"What do you think that drone was all about?" she asked.

"I don't know, but I think the whole family needs to know about it. It could just be someone playing with it and hiding when they spooked the cattle. But we're pretty isolated out here so that seems a little odd. Best not to speculate and wait to get everyone's opinion tonight." He looked down at his phone and sent a group text.

"But I like to speculate," she whined.

"Then you can do so at the family meeting."

"What if I can't make it to the meeting?"

"It's at dinner."

"Still. I might be busy." She turned her back to him and started to sashay away.

He growled, grabbed her arm and whirled her around to face him while simultaneously backing her up against the cupboard.

It was a smooth move while at the same time kind of cave-manish, and she liked it. A lot. "You've got some hidden talent with those actions."

"Woman, you have seen nothing yet." His voice was rough and sent a thrill through her.

He pressed up against her and she could feel his body responding to hers. She reveled in her femininity and rubbed against him, which caused him to groan and harden even more. So, she did it again.

"Now, stop that Alyssa. We're in the kitchen and anyone could walk in at any moment."

"Do we need to go back out to work?"

He blinked at her question, like maybe his brain couldn't catch up. "No, if they need us they can call me."

"Good. Then let's take this to a more private area." She rubbed against him again just to remind him what she was talking about.

He sucked in a breath. "Where did you have in mind?"

"My room."

"I don't think that's a good idea."

"Your room, then."

Beau groaned. "Alyssa, are you sure you want to go down this path?"

She thought back to her time in the truck and the fears she hadn't allowed herself to think of. She thought about what might have happened. She remembered seeing the truck he was driving come into view and the relief she had felt. "Yes, Beau. I am certain. I want to be with you in every way. I want to celebrate life. And I want to do it with you. Now."

"If you put it that way. I can understand your thoughts. I was feeling pretty stressed when I couldn't contact you and that spring storm was hitting us."

"Is that what we're calling it? That blizzard was a spring storm?"

He laughed. "Yes, that's what it was. A winter blizzard is much worse. Can last for a day or a week and dump several feet of snow." Glancing at her he asked, "So, do you have any supplies in your room?"

"Supplies?"

"Protection."

"Oh. No. I guess I don't." Darn it, how could she forget something so crucial? He was going to think she was an idiot and too young. It wasn't her fault—she hadn't thought she was coming to the Rockin' K to have sex, she thought she was coming to work. It wasn't her fault he was so hot, and she'd gotten caught in a blizzard and had been scared to death. It wasn't her fault she hadn't been off the ranch since she'd arrived weeks ago. Well, maybe that part was her fault, and her work-a-holic-ness, but still.

"My room, then."

She grinned at him. "Yay. Let's get moving before someone comes in and distracts us." Grabbing his hand, she tugged him out of the kitchen toward the bedrooms.

CHAPTER 22

*B*eau wasn't sure this was the wisest course of action, but he needed the life-affirming activity almost as much as she did. He wasn't used to worrying about people. The animals, yes. But people? Not so much. Everyone on the ranch had lived in Colorado all their lives and knew the score. Which was part of the reason he'd been worried about Alyssa—she didn't. But if he were honest that wasn't the only reason. He felt different about her than he did everyone else. Like she was vital to his life in some way. He didn't understand it, but somehow, she was in a category all her own. She mattered and the thought of her in danger had made him a little crazy. He was glad the twins had been in the truck with him when she didn't answer right away. He'd had to stay calm and rational with them being there, instead of going off like a crazy person to hunt for her in blizzard conditions. Yes, he knew the ranch as well as anyone but that didn't mean he could see hidden trouble when it was white out conditions—he didn't have x-ray vision. But he was afraid that if the twins hadn't been with him he would have risked it to find her and make sure she was safe.

He bumped into her when she stopped a few steps from his door. Was she having second thoughts? God, he hoped not.

"What's wrong, Alyssa?"

She let go of his hand and looked down at the floor. "Am I being too pushy? You don't seem to be fully engaged."

"What? Yes, I am. Why would you think that?"

She blushed. "I don't know which room is yours, and you're not leading the way. I've been dragging you along. If you don't want to do this…."

He pulled her in and kissed her long and slow. He pulled her hips in close, so she could feel what she did to him, as he hardened further. She hummed and rubbed her stomach and femininity against him, which made his eyes cross from pleasure.

"Okay. So you're on board, but I still don't know which room is yours and *umph*."

She couldn't say anything else as he hoisted her over his shoulder and carried her into his room, kicking the door shut behind him and firmly locking it. He walked across the room and dumped her on his bed, following her down. He had his mouth on hers before she could even bounce.

ALYSSA WAS glad Beau was finally taking charge. She didn't mind leading the way, but she'd felt he was just following along earlier. When she'd stopped as she reached the end of the hallway where Beau's room was, and he'd bumped into her like he wasn't paying attention, she'd started thinking that maybe he didn't really want to have sex with her. That she was being too forward, dragging him to bed. She had begun to feel mortified at her actions and had let go of his hand, thinking maybe she would just slink off to her room.

But he'd acted surprised and had kissed her stupid out in the hall. His body had been interested in her, for certain. Then, he'd gone all caveman hoisting her over his shoulder like a bag of feed, which had knocked the air out of her but had given her a nice up-close view of his ass. A very nice view, indeed.

She hadn't even seen a glimpse of his room before she was flat on her back with a hungry man on top of her, kissing the stuffing and sense out of her. She wrapped her arms around his neck and spread her legs so he could climb between them, which he did not hesitate to do.

"You taste like pure sin, woman. I can't get enough of you," he muttered as he kissed his way down her throat, nipping at her ear on the way.

She shivered and was heating up to an inferno. Wetness pooled between her legs as he rubbed against her.

"Beau, less clothes." She started pulling the shirt out of the top of his pants. She wanted skin.

He sucked on her neck for a moment which made that inferno leap higher, then he pulled back and yanked the snaps open on his shirt. A woman had to love cowboy-fashioned shirts. He tossed it aside and pulled off his T-shirt and tossed that aside and there was all that gorgeous skin and beautiful muscles—and she wanted her hands on every inch, or maybe her mouth, or both would be best. She reached for him, but he pulled her up and removed her flannel shirt and T-shirt and even her sports bra. And then they were skin to skin, and that was outstanding.

All that warm male skin was pressed against her and there was a little bit of friction from the smattering of hair on his chest. She moaned in delight—the sound just wouldn't stay inside.

He kissed her until they had no breath, tongues mating and dancing. When they finally had to get some oxygen, he kissed over to her ear and then down her neck stopping to bite lightly in the soft place where shoulder meets neck and then kept going lower—kissing the tops of her breasts and licking in the valley between the two. Coming closer to where she wanted that hot mouth but not quite getting there.

She whacked him on the shoulder. "Stop teasing."

He grinned up at her, and then pulled her nipple into his mouth and sucked hard. She about went off like the fourth of July and dug her nails into his back. She had short nails, so she knew she wouldn't draw blood, but he might have some bruises tomorrow.

He pinched the other nipple between two fingers and she squirmed. "Yes."

He bit lightly on her nipple and dragged it out of his mouth, his teeth scraping lightly. Then, he moved over to the other breast to give it some attention.

She thought she was going to come right then and there, the feelings were that exquisite. Fire raced in her blood and she could do nothing but thrash on the bed as he pleasured her breasts with his tongue and teeth and lips. The man had some serious skills, but she needed more. She wanted him to fill her, complete her, make her his.

"Still too many clothes," she managed to gasp out.

He looked up at her in delight, as both hands went to her breasts, massaging and squeezing them and pinching the nipples which furled into tight buds from all the attention. Then, he looked lower and started kissing and nibbling his way down her torso until he got to her jeans. He unbuttoned the top button, pulled it open, and kissed the V of skin uncovered. Dear God, he was going to kill her.

The zipper was lowered click by click, so slowly she was certain she would go mad before he got it unzipped all the way. He pulled the sides apart and kissed the skin above her panties. She moaned and squirmed beneath the onslaught.

She lifted her hips off the bed and he obliged her by pulling her jeans over her hips and down her legs. He tossed them aside along with her socks and then kissed and nibbled his way up her leg starting with her toes. When he was nearing the apex, he stopped and moved to the other leg doing the same thing. She thought about kicking him for tormenting her, but it was too amazing to stop.

The second time, when he reached the top of her leg, he nuzzled her and breathed deep, which made her want to scream with pleasure.

"Beau, for God's sake, you're killing me."

He looked up at her with fire in his eyes; the lust she saw there about did her in. "Just savoring you, lovely lady. Enjoying. Every. Single. Inch. Now, just lay back and take it."

He started pulling her panties down with his teeth, but when they got far enough to free her he ripped them off with his hands and tossed them on the floor. Then, he spread her legs and she about died when he licked her. Lightening shot through her whole body as the man teased and tormented her most sensitive flesh.

She gripped the blankets and held on for the ride. She was completely incoherent with ecstasy as he pleasured her to mindlessness. She lay there panting as he stood and divested himself of his jeans, shorts, and socks. He pulled a foil packet out of the drawer, ripped it open, and rolled the condom on, while she watched in anticipation of having all that manhood inside her filling up all the empty places.

She managed to whisper, "Come here and give me that."

He grinned. "Your wish is my command."

He climbed on the bed, got between her legs, and filled her with one long stroke. It was magnificent. Her body stretched to accommodate his girth, and she hummed in pleasure, lifting up so he slid in deeper.

He growled and started moving in smooth even strokes,

loving her again and again, hitting a spot deep inside that sent jolts of lightning through her body. She wrapped her legs around his hips, locked her ankles, and met him stroke for stroke. She felt her body wake up and come to attention as he loved her. It was the most amazing thing she'd ever experienced. She'd had sex a few times before, but nothing in her past experience compared to this. She didn't even have any words to describe what he was doing to her body—she just knew she never wanted him to stop.

Her body started gathering for release and she wasn't sure she could handle all the sensations he created.

He groaned. "Come for me now, Alyssa." And her whole being exploded into a shower of light that filled the whole room with shimmers. She barely felt him stiffen and growl with pleasure as he joined her in release. When her body and soul finally coalesced back together, and she could think again, she realized Beau was still inside her and he was smooshing her into the mattress. It was a wonderful feeling of togetherness and she would have loved to stay that way, except the man was heavy and she was having trouble getting enough oxygen. A few seconds later he rolled, off her— pulling her with him, so she ended up on top.

"Mmm a soft Alyssa blanket."

She smiled at his silliness but didn't have the energy to speak yet. She tucked her head on his shoulder and wrapped her arms around his waist and snuggled in.

BEAU WAS PERFECTLY content to lie in his bed with Alyssa draped over him for the rest of the day, or week, or month. Not that they had the luxury to do that, but it was a pleasant thought. Her skin was so soft, like velvet, and she smelled heavenly. She was curvy and plush in all the right places, but there were muscles under that softness he admired. He already knew she was a hard-working woman, that so far, had never shied away from anything that needed doing.

She had a delightful sense of humor and was sweet and kind without being a pushover. She'd put him in his place when he needed it, but she'd not done it in a public manner. She was good with the hands, the family, and the animals. He'd seen her slip a few tasty morsels of food to the old yellow mutt that lived in the kitchen. The dog was too old to work anymore, but he'd been a good steady working dog, and no one had the heart to put him down. So, he lived in the kitchen on a soft bed. It wouldn't be long before he passed, but they all hoped he did it quietly in his sleep.

She worked well with the cattle, the horses, and the dogs. She'd even gone out to see the bulls a time or two and they appeared to—if not cuddle up to her—at least tolerate her. Most of the men couldn't get as close to the bulls as she did. She was such an asset and having her wrapped around him— as she was—made him yearn for her to stay with them.

CHAPTER 23

*A*lyssa wasn't sure she would ever be able to move again. She was totally wrung out, her muscles nothing but jelly. She couldn't say for sure if her bones hadn't liquefied in the heat they had generated, but Beau's skin smelled like heaven and she wanted to lick him like a popsicle—especially all those delicious chest muscles and abs. Maybe she would just take a little taste. Without moving she reached out her tongue and licked his collarbone. Mmm tasty.

"Did you just lick me?" he asked.

"Maybe."

"Why?"

She licked him again in a little larger spot. "Because you taste delicious."

"That's just silly."

She raised off him and looked him in the eye. "It is not, and I am going to do it all over and you are just going to lay there and take it."

"I am?"

"Yes, you are. It's my turn to enjoy your body like you did mine, so prepare to be ravished, cowboy."

He laughed and spread his arms wide. "Do your worst."

"Oh no, I'm going to do my best." Her body seemed to have come back to its normal state with the idea of tormenting Beau. She started by outlining his chest muscles with her tongue and lips. Grazing his nipples with her teeth she could feel his body tense. A shudder ran through him when she bit down lightly on one. So, she gave the other the same attention and finished by kissing her way down the middle of his chest to his abs, where she reveled in all those muscles. As she paid attention to each one it jumped beneath her lips and tongue. Alyssa was patiently giving each muscle her attention while trying to decide if she wanted to follow that path of hair straight down the middle of his body to the promised land. Or if she wanted to devour those V-shaped muscles and deep grooves that ran from his hips down to that same enticing area, which seemed to be growing under her ministrations.

She planned to take that magnificent organ into her mouth and pleasure the man until he begged for mercy. This girl was no goody two shoes, and he was going to be well aware of that fact by the time she finished with him.

BEAU WAS DYING. Her hot mouth and that wicked tongue were about to drive him straight up the wall. He'd never realized his chest or abs were so sensitive until she started licking and kissing him all over. She even occasionally took little bites and then kissed the sting away. That delightful mouth kept heading south and his cock was totally on board with that idea. But he wondered if she would shy away from it once she got down there. She was taking her sweet time and his whole body was on fire.

She seemed to be following the path of hair straight down his body until she was almost to the place he wanted her most. Then, she stopped and went back up to his right hip and started licking and kissing the muscle that ran from his hip to his groin. When she got almost all the way down a second time, she went to the other hip and did the same thing. He knew he was going to die from desire as she teased all restraint out of him.

Finally, she got back down to his cock, and did not hesitate one second when she took his balls in one hand, wrapped the other hand around the base of his cock, and slid her hot mouth over the head. He groaned and was certain his eyes rolled back in his head at the pleasure she was giving him. He was gripping the bed so hard he was sure there would be permanent indentations in the mattress from his fingers.

When his body started to move toward release he took hold of her shoulders. "Alyssa, stop."

She shook her head and kept at it.

"No, stop. I want to be inside you."

She stilled her movements like she was thinking about that idea. Then she lifted her head, looked at him and nodded. But before she left the area she gave his cock one last long lick that had his eyes crossing. Then, she shimmered up his body, got a condom out of the bedside table and rolled it on him with very slow deliberateness. Grasping at straws to resist his climbing orgasm—so he could be buried balls-deep when he shot his load—he started reciting cattle birthing records in his head.

She finished sheathing him and squeezed. "What are you doing?"

He grabbed her, flipped her on her back, and entered her

so fast he could only hope he hadn't been too rough on her. But he had no control left. None. Whatsoever. He'd been hanging by a thread before she'd started rolling on the condom. That thread had snapped.

∾

ALYSSA WAS STARTLED when Beau flipped her down on the bed and entered her in one forceful plunge. She grinned as she realized she'd pushed him beyond the breaking point. That had been her mission, to make him as crazed with lust as he'd made her earlier. Mission accomplished.

He was pounding into her and it was glorious. She'd worked herself into a highly fevered state while she was pleasuring the man, so his punishing pace was going to send her right over the edge, with no hesitation at all. Her body started to tingle just as he went stiff. Knowing that he was coming pushed her to completion. Her body milked his in perfect harmony.

When she could finally think again, she teased, "Hey, I wanted to be on top. You took over my turn."

He chuckled and rolled them onto their sides. "Sorry about that. You can be on top some other time when you haven't tormented me beyond control, naughty girl."

She grinned at him. "My plan worked perfectly, then."

"If you were trying to turn me into a raging beast with no control or finesse, then yes. You succeeded."

"You can have control and finesse elsewhere—I kind of liked the raging beast."

"In that case it was my pleasure."

His phone signaled with what she assumed was the meeting reminder. She looked over his shoulder at the clock on the night stand and groaned. "We've got about a half hour before we need to be downstairs for your dinner meeting and I need a shower first."

"Yeah, me too. I have an adjoining bathroom that we can use, but it connects to Adam's room, so you would have to be very quiet if we use it together."

She grinned at him. "I can be quiet."

He shook his head sadly. "I'm not sure I believe that. You've been rather vocal recently. It's a darn good thing I'm the end room or we might have given the entire family something to talk about."

She punched him on the arm. "I was not vocal."

He raised the pitch of his voice, "Oh, Beau. Yes, right there. Faster. Don't stop."

"*Hmph.* Well, you must have needed instruction, then," she said as she rolled away from him and got off the bed.

"Instruction, my ass," he growled and chased her to the bathroom.

She turned at the door and put a hand on his chest. "*Shh*, you have to be quiet so Adam doesn't hear. Make sure he isn't in there. We have to hurry or we're going to be late for dinner. No shenanigans."

Adam wasn't in the room, so they went in and had a quick slippery shower with some quiet giggling and very few shenanigans. But Alyssa wished with all her heart and soul they didn't have to rush. This was, by far, the best afternoon of her life.

CHAPTER 24

*B*eau and Alyssa reluctantly went down for dinner.
Grandpa K said, "Looks like you survived being out in the spring storm, Alyssa. That was some mighty nasty weather that blew in here so quick, with no warning."

Alyssa smiled at the grizzled old guy. If he thought it was nasty, then she didn't feel so bad. "It was kind of scary out there all alone with my phone busted. Mostly because I didn't know what to expect, since I couldn't Google to see the norms for this area."

Travis looked at Beau. "I assume this family meeting you called has something to do with this."

"Yeah, but there's more to it than I expected. Let's get some food on our plates and then we can discuss it."

They passed around platters of chicken fried steak, and bowls of mashed potatoes, gravy, and vegetables. Cade tossed everyone a dinner roll, which made Tony hoot with laughter. When everyone had a plate full of food, Emma said grace, and the eating began.

Beau had a couple of bites before he put down his fork

and started relaying all the information he'd gathered that afternoon. Starting with why Alyssa was out by herself and had been detained long enough for the snow to start without her noticing and finishing with the conversation with the hired hands. Alyssa added any details he missed as he was talking.

When they were finished with the telling, Beau and Alyssa picked up their forks to eat while everyone discussed what they'd said.

Travis said, "I can't imagine why a drone would be that far out on our property. It doesn't make sense."

Chase said, "Maybe it was a kid and when he spooked the cattle he hid."

Cade answered his twin, "A kid from where? We don't have any kids near us."

Adam tapped his fingers on the table. "Maybe it was a long distance experimental drone whose programming went haywire and it got lost."

Drew shook his head. "That would have to be a very long-distance drone if it started on public property."

"Maybe it was someone spying on us," Emma whispered.

"Who would spy on us? And even more importantly, why would they want to?" Meg said, shaking her head at her daughter.

"I don't know. Didn't you do some experimental artificial insemination this year, Beau?" Emma asked.

Beau nodded. "I did, but nothing that is spy-worthy. Plus, I plan to publish and present my findings at the seminar next year at the college."

Alyssa was surprised to hear Beau was planning to present. It was kind of a prestigious honor to be invited. "You're going to be at the AI seminar next year?"

Beau shrugged. "Yeah, if I get some good data to present."

Alyssa smiled. She would see him again before Christmas, and that made her happy. "Cool."

He grinned back at her.

Travis interrupted their mutual sappy-expression sharing. "Regardless of why they were on our property, we need to keep an eye out for those drones."

Beau looked at his father. "I told Lloyd and Kent to send a family text if they saw them again, but we should probably let all the hands know. Word will pass slowly through the ranks, but who knows how the message will get scrambled."

"Like playing telephone," Emma laughed.

"I'll send a text to them all," Adam volunteered.

∼

BEAU WAS ABOUT to piss Alyssa off, but it had to be said. "I also didn't like Alyssa being alone. I think we need to work on our buddy system a bit more." Alyssa started to interrupt, but he held up his hand and continued, "It's not really wise for any of us to be alone when out checking on the cattle and helping them during birthing season."

Travis nodded. "I agree, the plan is to have you and Alyssa rove with the pair working and assist as needed, not go off and check the rest of the herd alone."

"But if I hadn't been there…."

Travis continued, "Yes, it was a good thing you were, but maybe if you had stayed with the pair and helped them finish the births they were recording, all three of you could have gone out and helped deliver the too-large calf."

"Or it might have been too late," she said stubbornly.

"A possibility, but you or Beau, or any of our other hands, are more important than one heifer and calf," Travis said pointedly. "Adam, add that to your text. No one goes alone."

"Yes, sir."

Beau could tell Alyssa wasn't happy with the decree, but it wasn't about her, exactly. It was about anyone being out alone. And it wasn't because she was some simpering female, because she wasn't that in any way. It was a precaution all of them needed to take.

He noticed Adam frowning at him and wondered what that was about. The twins seemed to have some kind of private joke between them.

Alyssa said, "I'll need a new phone. Is there somewhere in town I can get one?"

Emma clapped. "There is, and I'll take you there tomorrow morning. Tony and I could use a distraction. With everyone working so hard on the cattle, we're lonely, aren't we Tony?"

Tony just grinned at everyone at the table, enjoying the attention focused on him. Beau would have been happy to take Alyssa to town, but it probably was a better idea to let Emma take her. Just in case there was a birth that needed to be attended to.

"Any other business that needs to be addressed at the dinner table?" Grandpa K asked, looking at each one of them. Everyone had a negative response, so they all went their separate ways. Alyssa and the twins were left with the cleanup per the assigned chore chart.

Beau decided to go check on his charges in the birthing barn. He hadn't looked at Dolly's leg yet. "I'll be in the barn if anyone needs me."

Adam said, "Me too," and followed Beau out the door.

When they got inside the barn, Beau turned to his brother. "Okay, what's got your panties in a twist?"

"You slept with her." Adam put his hands on his hips and glared.

"There was no sleeping involved."

"Dammit, Beau. What in the hell are you thinking? She's only here for a short time and you're like her teacher right now. Don't you have to turn in a report on her and her work here? How are you going to be truthful if you're involved?"

"I am going to give her a glowing report because that's what she deserves. She hasn't done one single thing wrong and has been an asset. She's worked hard and learned more than anyone else on this ranch has about the cattle. She even has some theories on some of the statistics and they make a hell of a lot of sense. I plan to execute her ideas when we breed again. And none of that has anything to do with my relationship with her."

"What about going off on her own, getting caught in a storm, and endangering herself?" Adam challenged.

Beau frowned. "That could happen to anyone and we need to be more diligent about our buddy system, anyway. I don't want the hands splitting up like Lloyd and Kent did. They should have called in for more help."

"I don't disagree with you on that, but I still don't like you hitting on Alyssa."

Beau nodded. "I get that, and it wasn't really me hitting on her. She was feeling revved up after the fear from the storm and needed to vent that somehow."

"More adrenaline than attraction? Is that what you're saying? You just happened to be handy?" Adam asked sarcastically.

Beau huffed. "No, we've had a spark since day one—we've just been ignoring it. Pushing it to the side, to do our jobs."

"I would have voted that you continue to do your jobs."

"Oh, don't worry big brother. We aren't going to let the cattle suffer for our relationship," Beau said tightly.

"I didn't mean it that way. I know that both of you will put the cattle first, and no harm will come to the cattle."

"Thanks for the vote of confidence."

"I just hope to hell you know what you're doing."

Adam left Beau standing there wondering if he did know what he was doing. But what was done was done and he was going to own it. And maybe even revel in it—he'd never before connected with anyone like he did with Alyssa.

CHAPTER 25

*A*lyssa carried dishes to the sink to rinse before putting them in the dishwasher. Chase and Cade were covering the leftover food to put in the fridge. She finished loading what she had and turned to go get more, only to find a wall of twins between her and the table. They both had identical smirks on their faces.

"What are you doing?"

"You can't hide it from us," Cade said.

"We've got you figured out," Chase said at the same time.

"What do you two smarty pants think you have figured out?"

Cade pointed at her. "You had sex with our brother."

Chase nodded. "Yeah, it's written all over your face. And his."

"You guys have extremely vivid imaginations," she said primly.

"Nope, not really. But we do have eyes in our heads and you two were making mushy faces at each other most of the meal." Chase gave her the sappiest smile she'd ever seen.

She laughed. "I think not. We did not have that stupid expression on our faces."

Cade elbowed Chase. "Maybe not, he looks like an idiot. But you're not getting off the hook that easily. Admit it, you had sex with Beau."

"I admit nothing. Now, let's get this dinner cleaned up. I've got things to do."

"Like play kissy face with Beau?" Cade chided.

She rolled her eyes at them. "No. Like emailing my family so they don't panic when they can't get in touch with me."

Their humor dropped immediately. Chase nodded. "Oh, yeah, we don't want your father sending out an all-points bulletin."

"No, we don't."

"But, we still aren't buying your Little Miss Innocent act one bit." Cade pointed at her.

She raised an eyebrow. "I never once said I was innocent."

They barked out a laugh and she gave them a sly smile.

They quickly finished the cleanup and Alyssa went to her room to fire up her laptop—because if she didn't let her dad know soon about her broken phone, he would panic, no doubt. As she booted it up she wondered how long Beau was going to be in the barn and if he would come to her after, or if she could sneak down to his room. She wished her phone wasn't broken so she could send him a provocative text or two.

But first, she had to reassure the parental unit and while she was at it she might as well include the whole family and Rachel. She typed up a breezy email about how a heifer had head butted her for helping with a birth and her phone had gone flying. She conveniently did not mention that she was alone in a blizzard at the time. Although she did tell them about a sudden storm sweeping in that had not been on the radar at all. She told them she was going into town tomorrow to get a new phone and she would text them when she was up and running again.

She heard back from all of them with cute notes and news about their day. Except from her step-mother, Ellen, and her best friend Rachel—they both knew her too well. They promised not to tell anyone else, but asked what had happened in the blizzard. She gave them a bit more information, but still not the whole story. Each one said they would let it go for now, but she was spilling when she next saw them. She laughed and warmed at the thought of people loving her and knowing her well enough to notice when she was hedging. She guessed her father might also not quite believe her, but he knew he could get it out of Ellen if he was worried. And Alyssa was okay with that.

BEAU CHECKED ALL the cattle and calves. They were doing fine. There were hired hands in the barn to make sure nothing was needed in the night. He went into Dolly's stall and realized her leg was pretty much completely healed and she could go out into the pasture with no problems. But she seemed perfectly happy in her stall and was glad to see him, so he decided she could stay inside until it got a little warmer out, or they needed the stall for another animal. He spent some time with her giving her a rubdown and some extra attention. He knew it was kind of silly for a cattle rancher to have a cow as a pet, but he didn't really care. He'd raised her, nursed her, and tended to her wounds. She liked his company and he liked hers.

After spending some time with Dolly, he worked on the birthing records for a bit and got those up to date. They would still need to go out and find the transposed calf and get his tag fixed up—but that was a job for daylight hours. He didn't have anything else to do and finally realized he was stalling, so he didn't have to go to the house. Because where he wanted to go was Alyssa's room, but where he *should* go was his own.

He didn't know if Alyssa would want him to come to her room, or if she was glad to be rid of him. But what if she did want him to come and he didn't? Would that hurt her feelings? Maybe this is what Adam meant about knowing what he was doing. Well, he didn't know, thank-you-very-much. He wished she had her phone, so he could text her and hint at joining her.

"Well, hell."

"So, are you just going to sit out here all night, cowboy?" Alyssa said softly. And still, it had startled him so bad, he thought he might fall out of the chair.

"I was trying to determine where to go next," he admitted.

"My room would work just fine since I stole some of your condoms—or yours would, too. I'm not adverse to walking down the hall."

His heart, mind and body relaxed. "So, you aren't sick of me? You want me to join you?"

"Of course. Now, come on, you're burning nightdark."

"Nightdark?"

"It's the opposite of daylight and you're wasting it sitting out here alone when you could be spending it with me."

He grinned, took her by the hand, and reeled her in for a long slow kiss. "Better?"

"Much, but I'm not getting naked in the barn office, so let's get a move on, cowboy."

"Yes ma'am, at your service," he drawled.

"Good, because I have plans for you."

They walked hand in hand out into the crisp night air, she stopped and looked up at the stars. "So beautiful, they look a little different here than they do at home, but not a lot. We both live in areas without a lot of ambient light. I'm further north than you are here, so it's a little different view."

Beau looked at the stars and thought of when she would be back looking at that little different view and his heart hurt, just a little, at the thought.

CHAPTER 26

*A*lyssa woke alone, which was disappointing, but she supposed it was for the best. They didn't need to flaunt it in front of the family that she and Beau were tearing up the sheets together. Some of them might think it was awkward or unprofessional of them. Or they might even think she was too young or not mature enough to be with him. She was just an intern and he was a fully certified veterinarian. She didn't plan to become a full veterinarian—sure, she'd looked into it, but another four or five years of college did not sound like something she wanted to do.

Even one more year to get her master's degree seemed like a lot. She was enjoying getting her hands dirty, so to speak. She loved working with the cattle and the calves, helping with difficult births. She didn't even mind the branding, dehorning, and castrating that was an inevitable part of all cattle ranches. She'd learned that as a child, when she'd seen it the first time and had been horrified. Her father had sat her down and explained that if a ranch had too many bulls it was dangerous, as bulls could get cranky. She'd seen a bull get cranky a time or two and knew her father was right.

It still wasn't her favorite part of the process, but cattle were raised to eat and that, as they say, is that.

She decided she better get moving because she was pretty sure little Tony got up early and would be raring to go to town. He still took an afternoon nap, so they needed to be done with their errands and back in time for that. As she moved to get out of bed a crinkle sounded and she looked to find a note from Beau. *Aww how sweet.* It just wished her luck on the phone hunting and replacement and he told her he'd see her when she got back. He had a strong bold handwriting and seeing it made her smile. She folded it carefully and put it in her wallet.

When she got downstairs, Tony was indeed raring to go. She heard Emma say, "Now calm down, Tony. We'll go when Alyssa is ready and not a moment earlier."

Tony yelled with joy when she walked into the kitchen. "Lyssa, you ready?"

Alyssa laughed. "Just let me grab a muffin and a cup of coffee, in a travel mug of course, and then I'll be ready."

"Yay. Hurry, Lyssa. Burning daylight."

She laughed again and hurried.

Tony chattered all the way to town, pointing out trees and cattle and birds. Alyssa looked at Emma. "Is he always this excited about going to town?"

Emma rolled her eyes. "No, but he asked me where we were going in town and I wasn't thinking when I answered, to the phone store."

"Why does he like the phone store?" Alyssa thought it was a little odd to have a child so excited about looking at electronics.

"It's not the actual phone store. It's what's next to it, which is the D-R-U-G store."

"Still not getting it."

"It's an old-fashioned D-R-U-G store, which means it has

a soda fountain and C-A-N-D-Y—a whole buffet of it. Every kind you can possibly imagine. It's like kid heaven. I have a list to buy for everyone at the house, so we'll probably end up spending more time there than doing everything else added together."

Alyssa was shocked. "Everyone in your family asked you to buy them something at this buffet of C-A-N-D-Y?"

Emma nodded solemnly. "Every. One. Plus, some of the guys that live on the property found out we were going and texted me their orders."

"Seriously?"

"Oh, yeah. Everyone is very serious about C-A-N-D-Y."

"Mama, why are you spellin' candy?" Tony asked.

Emma started, "Tony what makes you think I'm doing that?"

"You been teachin' me my letters and those are the same letters I see'd at the drug store, next to the phone store, where all the candy is."

Emma shook her head.

Tony continued, "I love candy so I learned to spell it for my Santa list next year."

Alyssa laughed, and Emma groaned. "I thought it was good to teach him his letters. I thought he was too little to use them to spell things."

Alyssa patted Emma on the arm. "My little sister, Beth, taught herself to read when she was still in kindergarten because some dumbaaa…, uh dum-dum, bought her a bird encyclopedia and we all hated reading it to her because it was so boring. So, she decided to learn to read it herself. By fourth grade she had an eighth-grade reading level. Looks like you might have the same thing in little Tony."

"I'm afraid you might be right, but how will I ever keep a secret now?"

"The same way parents all over the world do. They don't. Unless they're super clever and use code."

"Thanks, Alyssa. Thanks a lot." Emma shook her head.

Alyssa laughed. "My pleasure."

When they got to town, Emma pulled into a parking space right in front of the drug store and Tony about had a meltdown, he was so excited. Rather than make the little boy wait while she got a phone, Alyssa suggested that they go in to do all their candy shopping while she went in the phone store. Emma gave her a grateful smile and took the hopping Tony into the drug store.

It didn't take Alyssa long to get a new phone. She wanted one that was compatible with the memory card she had, so she didn't lose anything. That narrowed the choices and took the wind out of the sail of the salesman who would have been happy to sell her the latest and greatest. She got the newer version of her previous phone, the technician switched everything over, and she was on her way in about twenty minutes.

She went next door into the drug store, which was a marvel in itself. It had everything—from small kitchen appliances to handmade jewelry. Tourist souvenirs sat next to the farmer's almanac. There was a pharmacy in the back and a soda counter ran along one wall. She decided she could easily spend a week in the store exploring and come out flat broke. She looked toward the front of the store where she found Emma with a pile of candy that was nearly as big as Tony.

Alyssa laughed as she walked over to her. "You weren't kidding."

"No, I wasn't. I might need a wheel barrow to get this all into the car and then into the house," Emma said sadly. "Tony is still debating his selection."

Alyssa looked, and sure enough the little boy was carefully examining the candy buffet. She loved that term, candy buffet. "Maybe I can help."

"Good luck, then."

Alyssa went over and knelt next to Tony. "So, what are you thinking, big guy?"

"Tryin' to decide if I want chocolate or gummy bears."

"Which one do you like better?" she asked.

"I really like chocolate, but I chomp it, and then it's all gone. Gummy bears are not as yummy as chocolate, but I can't chomp them. I gotta chew and chew, so I have them longer."

"I see your dilemma. Did you know that they have chocolate coated candy that has a gummy center, so it takes you longer to eat it?"

Tony looked at her wide eyed. "They do?"

"Yes, some places even have chocolate-coated gummy bears, but my personal favorites are these chocolate-coated raspberry jellies."

He thought for a minute and said, "I like raspberry jelly on my toast."

"Well then, how about you give these a try. And if you aren't happy with them, I'll come back and buy you something else and I'll eat these."

"Yay, I want to try them." He hopped up and down and clapped his hands in glee.

Alyssa took two packages of the candy, because now she wanted some, too. She turned to take Tony to his mother and noticed Emma talking to a guy that looked angry. Alyssa didn't know whether to keep Tony occupied and away from the discussion or backup Emma. She was relieved when Emma and the woman behind the counter spoke sharply to the man and he finally walked away, still angry.

Alyssa took Tony to the counter. Emma's hands were shaking as she paid for the candy. Alyssa said gently, "Why don't you take Tony to that park across the street. I'll load the candy in the car and join you."

Emma gave her a strained smile. "I'll do that." She waved her hand toward the woman behind the counter. "This is Katie, she's friends with the twins. Katie, this is Alyssa our intern this spring. Thanks for your help, Katie."

"Any time, Emma. Go on and take Tony to the park," Katie said.

Alyssa paid for her and Tony's candy. "So, you're friends with the twins?"

Katie was a short woman with brown hair that turned golden at the ends. "Yeah, we went to school together our whole lives. I wanted to wait until Emma got out of earshot before I said anything. See if you can convince her to get a restraining order on that jackass. He was being threatening. I'm a few years older than the two of them, and used to babysit him, so he backed down when I came to her defense. But I don't like what he was saying."

She nodded at the feisty woman. She was little, but she had a strong personality. "I'll give it a shot."

"Good. Let me know if I can help. Cade and Chase both have my number, or I'm here most of the time."

Alyssa said goodbye and then took all the purchases out and put them in the trunk of Emma's SUV. She didn't know what was going on, but clearly that guy had upset Emma and worried Katie.

Tony was busy playing on the slide and climbing all over the attached fun area while Emma watched him from a bench on the edge of the playground.

Alyssa went over and sat next to her. "Are you alright? I saw that guy harassing you."

"Oh, I'm sorry you had to see that. I dated that guy for maybe five minutes back in high school and now he thinks he can harass me about my son. He seems to think I cheated on him with Tony's father. I only went out with Nate twice before I realized he was an abusive ass and cut him loose. Tony was born a year and a half later, so anyone with any math skills at all can see it was long after I broke up with Nate. But he still harasses me every time he sees me. I'm just glad Tony was busy with you because he doesn't need to hear that kind of crap."

"Have you told your brothers about his abuse or gotten a restraining order?"

"No, I don't want any of the boys to kill him, and I thought Nate would get over it and move on. But after today, I'm considering a restraining order. He backed down when Katie told him to leave her store. I'm not sure he would have, otherwise. He seems to be getting more aggressive."

"I think it would be a good idea to make it official."

"Yeah, it might be time to do something. Tony is four years old, Nate needs to move on and leave me alone."

"Do you want to do that today? I can keep an eye on Tony."

Emma bit her lip.

"Go ahead. We can play here at the park. And then if you aren't back by lunch, I'll take him to that sandwich shop and feed him something."

"Alright. I think it's a good idea to get this taken care of. Tony likes grilled cheese, French fries, and milk. Or chocolate milk if he's being good. But no juice."

Emma walked off to take her SUV down the street to the sheriff's office. Alyssa hoped she was doing the right thing by encouraging Emma to get a restraining order. But no one should live under the harassment she'd seen from the guy.

CHAPTER 27

A little while later, Tony came running up. "Where's mama? I want to swing."

"Mama had to go take care of some things. Do you want me to push you in the swing?"

He nodded. So, Alyssa walked over to the swings with the little guy and got him settled in and gave him a small push.

"Bigger, Lyssa. Higher."

She put a little more strength into it so he went higher and he seemed to be happy with that, she didn't want to push him too high—she didn't know his strength or agility, so she was glad when he didn't ask for more. He was happy in the swing for about ten minutes and then wanted down to go on the flat merry go round thing. Fortunately, there wasn't a lot of kids at the park, so she put him into the middle with his legs straddling a bar and pulled him slowly around. He tried to talk her into faster, but she had no intention of going faster. She'd seen a lot of kids go flying off one of those things. One kid had broken his arm, and she'd seen a few other minor injuries from them. She had no intention of letting Tony be one of them. When he got tired of that, he went back to the slide and climbing structure for a while.

He came over to her and said, "Do you have any snacks, Lyssa? I'm hungry."

"How about we go over to the sandwich shop and I'll get you a grilled cheese?"

He looked longingly at the slide and then nodded. "I'm hungrier than a grouchy bear."

Alyssa laughed. "Then, let's go get some food for that grouchy bear tummy."

"Will mama find us?"

"Yes, I told her I would take you there to eat when you were ready."

"Yay." He grabbed her hand and pulled her toward the sandwich shop.

A waitress told them to sit anywhere they wanted, so they found a table near the window. It was a typical sandwich shop with kind of a retro feel—the tables were chrome and the chairs had red plastic seats. The waitress brought them a child's menu, some crayons, and a menu for Alyssa.

She asked what they wanted to drink and Tony immediately said, "Juice."

Alyssa shook her head. "Your mom said no juice. You can have milk or chocolate milk if you are good for me."

"I'm good, chocolate milk." Tony crowed.

Alyssa nodded. "Chocolate milk for my date, and I'll have unsweetened iced tea."

The waitress brought their drinks back and asked if they were ready to order. Just as they finished ordering, Emma came in and sat with them. "Jen, I'll have the club sandwich and a soda. I need both the sugar and caffeine."

Jen went off to get the soda and put in their order. Alyssa looked at Tony who seemed to be busy with his crayons and coloring all over his menu. So, she asked Emma, "How'd it go?"

"Fine, except it was Drake I talked to, and he'll probably let it slip to one of my brothers. Or in reality, is probably already on the phone to my dad."

Alyssa frowned. "He's a professional."

"Yes, but I'm like his adopted daughter, so he was already pissed off about it. If Nate isn't careful, he'll end up behind bars or something worse if my brothers or dad find out."

"Well then, he won't be out harassing women, will he."

"No, but my brothers have wicked imaginations, so I kind of feel bad for Nate if they decide to take it upon themselves to convince him to back off."

Alyssa shrugged. "Might serve him right."

BEAU WAS NOT HAVING a good day. There were small issues everywhere he looked and every time he had to do something, he wished Alyssa was by his side because she thought the way he did and he didn't have to tell her every damn thing he needed. Nothing he was doing was life threatening, but it was all taking twice as long as it would have with Alyssa. He was coming to depend on her more than he should.

He even caught himself wondering if he could tempt her into staying on and working with them. He knew she had plans for next year, but she was already such an asset that he would pay her to stay. The fact that they were extremely compatible in bed didn't hurt, either. He wouldn't mind exploring their relationship into the summer months. Not that they really needed two vets at that time of year. In fact, most of the time he wasn't a vet at all in the early summer— just a rancher, growing hay and checking fence lines. He would have an occasional stitch to put in, more often than not on a cowboy who let the barbed wire get away from him. Later in the summer he would begin the breeding program which, of course, Alyssa was very interested in. So, she might like to be around for that and they could put some of her ideas into practice.

She probably would want to go home for a while, but maybe she could come back in July and August for a while, before she went back to college. He would need to think about that, and maybe feel her out about the idea.

Finally, a dirt cloud filled the air where the driveway was and he hoped it was Emma, Alyssa, and Tony back from town. They would have had plenty of time for shopping and lunch by now, providing they hadn't gone clothes shopping —because that could take all day, but he didn't think Tony would be patient that long, anyway.

When Emma drove up with Alyssa and Tony, Beau felt like cheering. He knew he was being ridiculous—it had only been a few hours they had been apart, but it had seemed like forever. What in the heck was he going to do when she left? He figured he could handle it, because she wasn't supposed to stay then, and wouldn't be a few miles away in town. He tried to be casual as he went toward the car to help carry in their purchases.

Emma got out and collected a sleeping Tony, but Beau thought she looked kind of tense and he wondered why. Had the girls not gotten along? That didn't make sense—they were both easy going and fun to be around. He noticed Emma look at Alyssa and his fears on that score relieved as she mouthed the word *thanks*.

Alyssa went to the trunk and he joined her, so he could help carry in the mounds of candy Emma had bought for everyone. Alyssa smiled when he picked up all but one small bag. "Are you showing off your manly muscles, Beau?"

"Of course, and helping you carry in all this loot, little lady," he drawled in his best Texas accent.

She laughed as he hoped she would, but she looked a little tense herself. "What happened in town that stressed you girls out?"

Alyssa startled. "Is it that obvious?"

"It is to me. What happened?"

She looked around and whispered, "I don't think Emma wants me to say anything."

Beau frowned at that. "She's my baby sister, Alyssa."

"I know but she handled it and then took some precautions."

"Why does she need precautions? I'll just go ask her, unless you tell me. And then, we can decide what the best course of action is."

Alyssa sighed. "I'll tell you, but only because I think someone on the ranch should know in case it escalates."

"Okay, now you're scaring me. Just what the hell happened?" He put the candy back in the trunk and folded his arms.

"Nothing dreadful happened, but there's this guy Emma dated that harasses her about cheating on him with Tony's father. Emma said they'd broken up long before Tony was conceived, and the guy wasn't even in the picture. She said she only went out with him a couple of times, because he wasn't a very pleasant guy even then." She crossed her arms and continued. "Anyway, he was harassing her in the drug store. Fortunately, Tony was with me and didn't hear or see anything, and Emma got the jerk to leave. I suggested if he'd been harassing her for four years then he wasn't going to quit, and she should get a restraining order."

Beau's gut was churning and he was furious. No one was going to harass his sister and get away with it. Why didn't anyone know about this? Why hadn't she come to them for help? But rather than flip out he simply said, "Good."

"I watched Tony at the park while she went and talked to the sheriff."

"She told Drake?"

"Yes."

That helped him to calm down some. Drake knowing about it and watching out for Emma was a good first step. "Even better, do you know what the guy's name is?"

"Ned, or maybe it was Nate. Yeah, Nate."

"That sounds just like the weasel, but I don't trust him not to try something in retaliation. I think I better talk to my brothers and dad about this, so we can be on the lookout. Thanks for telling me, Alyssa. We don't want anything to happen to Emma or Tony."

"Yeah, that was my thinking, too. He didn't do much more than just mouth off, but they were in a public place. Do you think Emma will be mad at me for telling?"

Emma walked around to the back of the car and hugged Alyssa. "No, she won't, because she knows it's time to let everyone know. Besides, if Drake hasn't already called Dad, I'll eat my hat."

Beau said, "Police don't go around spilling stories."

"Except to his best friend since third grade, and the father of his god-daughter," Travis said as he joined the party and pulled Emma tight into his arms. "Nate better stand down or he's going to have the Kipling wrath poured out on his head."

Emma laughed through her tears then looked at Beau. "Told ya."

"We'll have a war council at dinner tonight to decide what measures to take to keep our girl and the little guy safe from assholes. Beau, spread the word. Emma, let's go have a talk. You can fill me in on the jerk's behavior."

Emma took Travis's outstretched hand. "Yes, Daddy."

Beau looked back at Alyssa. "Thanks for encouraging her to finally say something."

"You're welcome. Sometimes us girls need to stand on our own two feet, but it's nice to have family at your back." She rubbed her arms like they were cold. "Four years is too long to ignore the problem and think it will go away."

Beau pulled her into his arms to warm her or give her comfort or something. When she relaxed into him he kissed the top of her head. "Exactly. Now, let's get this loot into the house. It looks like you guys cleaned out the shelves," he teased her and tried not to think about how perfectly she fit in his arms.

CHAPTER 28

During dinner, the family talked about their ideas to keep an eye on Nate. After the initial furor died down, they made good plans that were not over the top in Alyssa's opinion. Although, she wouldn't want to be Nate if he didn't back off. Five brothers, a father, and a grandfather were a lot of people to have pissed off. But the real kicker was the mother bear. Meg was ready to fillet the man and serve him up to some hungry bears.

Meg said, "It's been a long cold winter, and one of the bears or wild cats would be happy with a little snack."

Everyone at the table shuddered at the thought and Drew said, "Mom, you can't say things like that. Now, if he goes missing, I'm going to have to investigate my own mother."

Travis smiled at his wife. "Don't worry, honey. I'll help you hide the evidence."

"Dad, not helping." Drew groaned.

Adam chuckled. "Maybe Nate is the one that needs protection. A whole lot more than Emma does."

Meg just shrugged. "He better watch his Ps and Qs then, and stop harassing my baby girl."

Emma grinned at her mother and Alyssa decided she was glad that Tony had eaten an early dinner and gone to bed before his normal time, because of his busy day in town. She thought he might be scarred to hear such talk.

Drew said, "You just let the law handle it. Nate might like to push women around, but going to jail is a whole other story. Drake served him this afternoon and let Nate know the department wouldn't put up with any BS from him, so he better keep his distance."

Meg nodded, but Alyssa didn't think Meg had changed her mind on the subject.

The candy hand-out turned into quite an event as each person ogled the other's candy and tried to convince Emma they had asked for it instead of the one that really had. Emma didn't budge on her list, even when Grandpa K tried to play the old and forgetful card. Emma just laughed and kissed his cheek. Every single adult acted more like a child than Tony had, and Alyssa found it quite entertaining.

When the candy euphoria died down, Beau and Alyssa went out to the barn to check on the animals, and then go over the births from the day. It was a crisp cold evening which surprised Alyssa after the warm day they'd had.

She shivered.

Beau pulled her in closer as they walked, and wrapped his arm around her. "If the skies are clear we often have warm days and cold nights. Nights end up being warmer with some cloud cover, because they hold in the heat."

"Thanks for the science lesson. Maybe I was just being dramatic, so you would hold me closer." She laid her head on his shoulder.

"No drama needed for that. I like holding you close. Just move on in anytime."

"Are you sure about that, cowboy? You might get tired of me all up in your grill all the time."

He stopped walking and pulled her completely into his arms holding her close. Then, he took her chin and looked into her eyes. "Yes, Alyssa. I am sure. I love the feel of you in my arms."

She shivered at the intensity in his eyes and the words he'd spoken almost reverently. She was getting lost in this man and she just didn't have any desire to stop the fall. She wished the semester would stop going by so quickly, but it was barreling on like a freight train.

BEAU FELT Alyssa shiver and decided he needed to get her into the barn, so she didn't get too cold. Neither one of them had thought to bring a coat with them because of the warm day. Not that they were going to freeze in the distance from the house to the barn, but still, it was foolish of him. He'd been focused on getting her away from his family and alone for a few minutes. He needed to get his mind in the game, rather than thinking of Alyssa all the time. He kept one arm around her and walked her quickly into the barn and into the office. He turned on the space heater and had her sit near it.

"I'll check the animals real quick. While I do that, bring up the database and we can talk about what happened while you were in town."

She nodded, and he walked out of the room as she typed in the password to the screen saver.

He chastised himself as he checked on the animals and made sure they had plenty of food and water, and none of them needed any care. He needed to make sure the animals came first before whatever this was he had going on with Alyssa. And he needed to make sure they didn't just go off like two idiots with no thought to the weather. It could still get nasty up in the mountains this time of year—they were moving away from snow and heading toward lightning storms. They could have either, so it was a volatile time of year and he needed to keep his head on his shoulders and not in his pants.

When he got back to the office he was sure he'd talked himself into some rationality, right up until he opened the door and saw her sitting in front of the computer, completely enthralled with the data on the screen. He groaned to himself and knew he was a goner. So, he decided that maybe he should work to compartmentalize his mind. Cattle and life during the day and Alyssa at night. He wasn't sure that would work, but he could give it the old college try. Besides that, him freaking out about forgetting a coat when they were going less than a dozen yards from the house was making a mountain out of a molehill. There were even some hoodies and jackets in the barn if they really needed them. He was turning into a basket case. Alyssa looked up at him and smiled. *Yep a basket case.*

~

ALYSSA WASN'T QUITE sure what Beau was doing standing in the door staring at her with a frown on his face. So, she decided to get him out of his funk with birthing questions.

"I was reading about your crazy morning. Nothing too critical, but it kept you hopping, didn't it?"

He smiled. "It did, and I missed you being by my side and anticipating my every need. I had help from some of the guys, but I had to tell them every little thing I needed. 'Get a threaded suture out of the compartment labeled suture. Carefully open the package without poking yourself. Hand me the needle. Clip the thread after each stitch.' It was exhausting, and it made me realize how easily you and I work together."

She grinned at him, enjoying the compliment.

He wagged his finger at her and teased, "So, no more going into town when every one of the cows giving birth decide to be contrary."

She said sweetly, "You just give me a schedule of those times and I will be happy to follow it. I am here to work, after all."

He groaned and stalked toward her. "Woman, you are going to be the death of me." He pulled her out of the chair, bent her over his arm and kissed the stuffing out of her. She was quite happy to comply with his kisses. Warmth filled her body and tingles shot through every limb. Her mind emptied as she enjoyed the sensations flooding her bloodstream.

When she was back on her feet with enough brain cells firing, she shook her head at him. "I'm here to work, not flirt… or kiss the boss."

He put his hands in his hair and pulled. Then he started muttering. "One little mistake. A guy makes one little mistake and does the woman let him forget it? No. She. Does. Not."

She laughed delightedly and poked him in the chest. "Don't you ever forget that, cowboy. Words are important, so you need to mind your tongue."

Beau shook his head. "Now, are we going to talk about the cattle or stand around flirting all day?"

"That's a tough decision." She turned toward the computer then looked back to him, then back toward the computer.

That time when she turned away from him, he swatted her lightly on the ass. "Brat."

She waggled her butt at him. "The boss is kind of strict. I don't think he would like me to goof around or flirt."

"Well, he might forgive you if you flirt only with him."

She frowned at him then turned away. Looking back over her shoulder she said, "Meany."

He guffawed. "I don't think we're going to get much done tonight. You're too feisty."

"Oh, goody. Let's go back to the house and have sex instead."

He lifted an eyebrow. "Race you."

She was off like a shot. He laughed and hit the lights on the way out of the room and then the barn.

She got to the door a second or two before he did and started crowing. "I win, I win."

"No, you didn't. We still have to get all the way to my room."

She shook her head. "No, we can't go racing through the house to your room."

"Why not?"

"We don't want to attract attention. Adam already glares at us and I don't believe for one minute he hasn't tried to talk you out of this."

Beau shrugged. "I don't give a hot damn what Adam thinks. This is my life and yours. His opinion is not important."

"Okay, I'll give you that, but we don't have to rub his nose in it, either."

"Fine, we can walk sedately to my room."

She nodded and fire lit her eyes. "Which means I won and you have to be my love slave."

His eyebrows rose. "Your love slave?"

"Yes, my *love slave*. You have to do everything I tell you."

"That doesn't really sound like a loss to me."

She pulled him in and whispered. "We'll see how you feel after I've had my way with you."

His whole body had frozen at the seduction pouring from

her lips. She hooked one finger in the belt loop on his pants and pulled. He followed her stupidly into the house and could barely function enough to get his boots off, there was so much lust running through his veins.

CHAPTER 29

*A*lyssa had no idea how she was going to follow up on all her seductive words out on the porch, but she needed to think of something and quick. She didn't have that much sexual experience to know how to pull off all her big talk. But, she'd mouthed off and now she needed to deliver. She wracked her brain, thinking about all the erotic books she'd read. Surely, there was something she could do that he wouldn't expect and that would rock his world, but what?

She'd read stories where the woman was the dominatrix, but those women always seemed a little mean to her. She wasn't into pain or anything truly kinky. Maybe if she didn't do anything new, but just commanded him to do whatever, that would be enough. If he was doing it by her will, rather than his, would that be sufficient to excite him?

Maybe—and since that's all she could think of, she would give it a go as they say. If it fell flat she would just confess that her mouth got ahead of her experience. She didn't think he would mind all that much, as long as they both had fun and enjoyed the experience it was worth it. He was following behind her, so she sashayed a little more than normal to give him something to look at. She heard him suck in a ragged breath and decided it was working.

She went into his room and he followed closely behind her. "Lock the door."

He snicked the lock closed.

"Now lock the door to the bathroom."

He did as he was bid.

"Good. Now take off your pants."

He lifted an eyebrow at that, but undid his belt and pulled it out of the loops and then un-buttoned his fly and pulled off his jeans.

"Good. Now your skivvies and socks."

He was now naked from the waist down and looked to be rock hard, although his shirt was hampering her view. But, she didn't have him take that off yet because it seemed kind of kinky to have him fully dressed on top and completely naked below.

"Pull your shirt up a little, so I can see that magnificent cock."

When he did, she licked her lips and saw it jump in response. She grinned inside and decided she wasn't doing too bad at her novice dominatrix bit.

She walked over to where he was standing and used one finger to run it up from the base of his cock to the top, where one drop of moisture pooled. She dipped her finger into the liquid and brought it to her lips to lick. She moaned at the delicious taste and Beau groaned and shut his eyes.

"Now, now. No shutting your eyes, my dear love slave."

"You're killing me, Alyssa."

She shook her head. "Nope, just teasing you a little. You can take your shirt off now, so I can see all those muscles."

He ripped his shirt off and tossed it to the side. She walked around him admiring his fully naked body. She squeezed his ass with one hand as she circled him. His body stiffened at her touch.

When she got back to the front of him, she touched one pec with one finger. "Very nice. Sit down on the bed."

He complied and she lifted one foot to the bed between his thighs. "Please take my sock off." As he pulled it off, her foot *slipped* and caressed his balls. She repeated the action with the other foot.

She moved in between his legs. "Take my shirt and bra off."

She thought she felt his fingers tremble as he took off her shirt and unfastened her bra.

"You may caress my breasts."

He didn't hesitate to do so. She was getting so turned on by his reactions that when he touched her breasts she thought she might go off like a Roman candle. Maybe she should speed things up a little, before she killed them both.

Beau worshipped her breasts, gently squeezing and weighing them in his hands. He pinched the nipples and smiled as they furled for him. "May I use my mouth?"

She nodded her agreement. She was getting as excited as he was. He'd never had a woman command him in the bedroom and it was a wild turn on. He didn't know how long he could stand it, but he was enjoying it while it lasted. He sucked on one nipple while he worried the other with his hand. Then switched sides.

She pulled back a bit, so her breast left his mouth with a pop. "Remove my jeans."

As he did as commanded, he noticed the crotch was damp.

"And the panties." Those weren't damp, they were drenched.

"Good. Now put on a condom, Beau."

"Yes ma'am," he drawled as well as he could, with his throat dry as a bone.

When the condom was on, she climbed up on his lap and drew him inside her body. He groaned at the pleasure and she purred. Her little love slave act had them both on the razor's edge.

She started moving on him and he worked hard to keep still until she told him differently. He was barely hanging on to his control by a thread.

She whispered, "Beau, make love to me." Then she wrapped her arms around his neck and her legs around his waist and held on tight as he did as commanded. It was glorious. He pumped into her and she met him stroke for stroke. When they broke, it was like fourth of July, Christmas, and New Years' all rolled in together. It was the most erotic experience of his life.

After they could think again, he said in a gravelly voice, "I'll be your love slave anytime, Alyssa. Any time at all."

She laughed and pulled him close. "I'll keep that in mind, Beau."

CHAPTER 30

*B*eau and Alyssa spent the next few weeks working hard during the day and loving hard at night. As the end of her internship grew closer Beau started thinking about ways to keep her on board—or maybe bring her back after the summer or even after her master's degree was complete.

One warm sunny afternoon, Beau decided it was time to put Dolly back out in the pasture. She'd been healed up for a couple of weeks and didn't need to be in the barn. Most of the other cattle were also out in the pasture. He walked into the barn and down to her stall.

"Hey, old girl. It's time to give up your cushy life and go out in the pasture with the rest of the herd. Summer's coming soon."

Dolly lowed and he rubbed her head and neck. "Now, you have to promise me that you'll be a good girl and stay away from any more beaver traps or anything else that could cause you trouble."

She bumped him with her nose and he took that as a promise to behave. Beau led her out of the barn, past the corral, and through the gate for the pasture. "You keep an eye on those young'uns while you're out there. You've got the most experience—I'm counting on you to keep those young mothers and their babies in line."

When they were well into the pasture, he stopped walking, and the cow stopped too. She just stood there next to him. Beau wacked her on the rump. "Go on now, out to the herd." Dolly rubbed against him one last time and meandered across the pasture. He watched her go for a few minutes and then decided to go find Alyssa.

Beau was a half hour early to the location he and Alyssa had planned to meet. He'd hurried through his work so he could join her earlier. She was already there at their designated place for the day too, so maybe she'd been just as eager. He noticed she was on her phone, so he just waited while she talked, drinking her in. She was animated and looked so beautiful it hurt. After a while, he started noticing her words.

"Being on campus is awesome." She paused and listened.

"Yes, of course an online degree is great, but you learn so much more with being hands-on and from the other people in the class with you. Some things are just easier to learn if you can touch them and see other people and their reactions. Videos and live interactions are great and so much better than what online degrees used to be. But there's just something so much better being on campus. Trust me on this."

Beau's gut clenched at her words. He'd been thinking about asking Alyssa to consider finishing her master's degree online. But clearly, she loved being on campus.

"No, it's not the same as being there. The online classes just lack something. I can't really describe it. But there is a huge difference. I think you learn so much more at the school."

He eased away without Alyssa seeing him. He needed to think about this revelation—or at least get his own emotions under control. He felt like he'd been kicked in the stomach or maybe the heart, by one of the bulls. He had half an hour before he needed to be back.

~

ALYSSA FINALLY HUNG up from talking to Rachel. That had been a long conversation. Rachel wanted to go to art school, but she was hemming and hawing. So, Alyssa had poured it on about how wonderful college was. She hadn't been lying to her friend—there was a wealth of knowledge that was gained by being on campus, both in life skills and classwork. Rachel had never lived on her own. She was still living with her family, in the same bedroom they had played Barbies in as little girls. Alyssa thought Rachel was longing for some independence. She would get that independence at college, but it was still a relatively closed and safe environment.

Rachel was a great photographer and had studied everything she could find online, but she wanted to try new things and push herself. Art school would do that, too. She hoped Rachel would give it a try. Alyssa, on the other hand, was ready to settle down and just work. She kept wondering if she really wanted to spend another year in school to get her master's degree. If she was honest with herself, which she tried to be, what she wanted to do was stay here on the ranch with Beau and work beside him. He was already trying some interesting ideas in reproduction and she felt like she could learn as much working with him during the breeding season as she would in school. He hadn't invited her to do so and she hadn't asked, but she might just do that and see where it led them.

She wondered where Beau was. She had hoped he would get finished early and meet her. She checked her Facebook and still no Beau. She checked her email and still no Beau.

She texted her family and still no Beau. He was late and she wondered if something was wrong. Finally, he sent her a text.

> Beau: Not going to be able to make it. Need to run
>   into town.
> Alyssa: Want company?
> Beau: Not this time. I'll see you tomorrow.
> Alyssa: Not tonight?
> Beau: No gonna be late.
> Alyssa: Late is better than not at all.
> Beau: Nope, see you tomorrow.
> Alyssa: Fine.

She put down her phone instead of throwing it like she wanted to. What was going on? They'd spent every night together since the first one. Sometimes, it had been late if he needed to do something that didn't include her, but he'd always shown up eventually. She didn't know what to think. When she'd seen him at lunch there was nothing different about him, so what had happened between then and now? Her stomach clenched, as dread reared its ugly head. She only had a couple weeks left. Was he breaking up with her?

She slowly walked to the house. She would just go to her room. When she walked in the kitchen, Grandpa K was sitting there having a cup of coffee.

"Hi, Grandpa K. I'm not feeling too great so I'm going to my room to lay down. Could you spread the word that I won't be down for dinner?"

"I can do that little lady. Is there anything I can do to help?"

She sighed and shook her head. She tried to smile but it felt more like a grimace. "No, I'll see you tomorrow."

Grandpa K frowned but didn't say anything else. Alyssa

took some cheese and crackers and an apple to her room, for a snack later if she had the desire.

~

BEAU KNEW he was being a chickenshit about this, but he just couldn't face her. Maybe he should just break it off. That way, neither of them would be hurt later. Or, would it be better to enjoy her the last few weeks they had together and let it end naturally with her leaving for graduation and the summer? He didn't know, and he had to think about it. He wished he had someone he could talk it over with, but he couldn't think of anyone. Adam was dead-set against the relationship. He hadn't talked to his parents about girls since he was fourteen. He had friends, but no one he was especially close to.

He'd told his grandfather he was going into town and wouldn't be back for dinner. But he had no real destination. He could go get some food or go to the bar, he supposed, but he wasn't feeling particularly social and he didn't really want anyone bugging him. Maybe he'd go for a drive to give him time to think things through. He probably shouldn't go too far in case there was some kind of an emergency on the ranch, but calving season was over and everything else was pretty well in hand, so he didn't expect anything—but you never knew. Alyssa could probably handle anything that was needed, but he was the vet, and it was his responsibility. So, he would stay in the area and not go any farther than Hot Sulfur Springs. He could grab something to eat at Mama B's Kitchen or the Glory Hole Café.

Beau drove around aimlessly for a couple of hours and still had no clue what he wanted to do about his relationship with Alyssa. He was tired of driving, still hadn't eaten, and he was just wasting gas, so he headed toward home. There would surely be some leftovers.

He walked in the kitchen and found his grandfather still sitting at the table, which surprised him. It wasn't that late yet, but his grandfather usually went to his room after dinner.

"Hi Grandpa, whatcha doing?"

"Waiting for you."

Beau went on full alert. "Why? Is there something wrong? Why didn't you text me?"

"Nothing is wrong with the stock. But I'm going to butt my old nose into your business. I'm thinking you did something to hurt Alyssa's feelings. Since you left, 'to go to town' and she went straight to her room and didn't come to dinner."

Dammit. He felt bad for hurting her feelings. She didn't deserve it. "I didn't mean to hurt her feelings. I just needed to think about some things and make some decisions."

"And did you do that?"

Beau shook his head. "I tried."

"I'm guessing this thinking had to do with Alyssa which is why she looked so sad. Did you consider talking to Alyssa about what you needed to think about?"

"No." Beau sat down at the table across from his grandfather. He felt too defeated to do anything else.

"Let me give you a piece of advice here, grandson. Always, and I mean always, talk things through. Nothing in existence can spin your life down the shitter faster than making assumptions, and then making decisions based on those assumptions. I had fifty-three years with your grandmother before she went to the great beyond. And I spent too many of the early years not talking things through and making bad decisions on false assumptions. Don't do the same, boy. You do know the word assume, stands for making an ass out of you and me?"

Beau grimaced and nodded. "I have heard that a time or two, yes."

"Then don't be an ass, and talk to the girl. And while you're at it, take some dinner up to her. I saved both of you a plate of food in the oven." His grandfather stood up and put his coffee cup into the dishwasher.

"Thanks, Grandpa."

"You're welcome, Beau. Goodnight." The old man walked out the door leaving Beau with his thoughts.

CHAPTER 31

*B*eau loaded up the warm plates and some iced tea onto a tray. He found brownies in a pan on the cupboard and figured chocolate would be good to have, just to be on the safe side. He managed to get to her door without spilling anything—he would never make it as a waiter, though.

He didn't know how to hold the tray and knock on the door at the same time, so he called out. "Alyssa? It's Beau. Can you open the door, please?"

He heard some rustling around and then the door opened just a crack. "I thought you weren't coming tonight."

"I changed my mind and brought you up some dinner. Can I come in?"

She looked down at the tray in his hands and sighed. "I suppose."

She stepped back and opened the door, and he was surprised to see her in one of his T-shirts paired with pajama bottoms that had big red lips all over them. There were fuzzy slippers on her feet and her hair was pulled up in a ponytail. He grinned at her and she scowled back at him.

"Don't you grin at me, Beauregard Kipling."

"You're wearing my T-shirt and big kissy lips pajamas. I like the connotation."

"Well, don't read anything into it, cowboy. I don't like being stood up with no explanation." She crossed her arms.

"Yeah. About that." He set the tray on her dresser, went to her, and took her hands in his. "I'm sorry about that. I was trying to sort through some things."

"And you had to stand me up to do it?"

"You're what I was trying to sort through."

"Oh, well, that makes sense I guess—but I still don't like it. You hurt my feelings and then I got ticked off because I didn't deserve for you to hurt my feelings, and then it circled back to hurt, around and around. It's not been a fun couple of hours, but I'm currently at the angry stage."

Beau rubbed the back of his neck. "So, Grandpa K told me to not assume anything and talk to you, so here I am."

"You do know that assuming only makes an ass out of you and me. So, what were you assuming?"

"I came to our meeting place a little early and you were on the phone, so I just waited while you finished your call."

She nodded. "Yeah, I was talking to Rachel. You weren't there when I hung up."

"No, I overheard you going on and on about how great college life was and how you can't learn as much doing an online course. And I understand that and agree. But...."

"But what?"

"But I'd been kind of thinking I didn't want you to go back to college. Selfishly, I was hoping I could talk you into finishing your master's degree online and staying here. And then when I heard you—"

He couldn't finish his thought because he had an arm full of woman. She'd flown at him like she had wings and was wrapped around him squeezing the breath out of him. Not that he was complaining, but he was not quite sure why she was stuck to him like cling wrap. He would ask her, but she had her mouth firmly planted on his, and his brain cells were being incinerated from her kiss.

Before he lost all ability to speak, he pulled his mouth off hers. "Alyssa, I'm confused."

She hugged him tightly as she laughed. Then she disengaged, slid down his body, and stepped back. He wished he'd kept his mouth shut, because he felt cold and alone.

She took his hand and pulled him over, so they could sit on her bed. "So, yeah. This was one of those, ass out of you and me times. I was talking to Rachel to try to convince her to go to art school, so the waxing on and on was to remind her of all the things a person could gain by being on campus. Which I have already done and learned. And to be frank, I'm kind of over it. I would be perfectly happy staying here on the ranch with you and getting my degree remotely. If they allow that kind of thing. I haven't asked because I didn't know if you wanted me to stay."

He laughed, and his heart lightened again like it had before he had overheard her conversation.

She poked him in the arm. "So, next time you eavesdrop, make sure you stick around to find out what I'm talking about and with whom. Because sometimes I tease Mike and make kissy noises at him. What would you have thought if you had caught that?"

He stiffened and then remembered Mike was her oldest brother. "I guess if I had known it was your brother Mike, it would have been fine, but if I didn't and thought it was some other guy? Yeah. I would have been freaked out by it."

"So, from now on, you ask first, right?"

He grinned at her. "Yes, ma'am.

She poked him in the chest. "And no more lying."

"I didn't lie."

"You said you were going to town." She put her hands on her hips.

He shrugged. "Oh, well, it was just a little lie."

"Big, little—they are all the same." *Poke.* "No." *Poke.* "More." *Poke.* "Lying." *Poke.*

"Got it." He rubbed his chest and gave her a wolfish smile. "So, do you want to eat first or fool around?"

Both their stomachs grumbled as if on cue. She laughed. "The stomachs have voted food first."

ALYSSA WAS STARVING. She hadn't realized her stomach was so churned up until Beau had shown up and they had talked through his leaving her high, dry, and confused. A guy disappointing her had never caused her to feel that way in the past —at least not that she could remember. She wondered why it had affected her so much. What was so different about this man that caused her heart so much trouble? Was this real love? She didn't think she'd ever been in love before. Oh, she'd been boy crazy a time or two, and she'd had some guys she had thought she loved, but when push came to shove she'd gotten over them pretty quickly. She wasn't sure that would be the case with this man.

"Your room is not very conducive for a picnic," Beau said looking around. "We have folding chairs and a folding table somewhere in this house, but by the time I track it down the food will be even colder than it is now."

"My room is just fine for a picnic. Bring the little desk over here by the bed to put the food on. I'll sit on the bed and you can sit in the chair."

"That works." He grabbed the desk in one hand and the

chair in the other and carried them over to the bed. Then, he got the tray off the dresser and put it on the little desk. "That's the tiniest desk I've ever seen."

They unwrapped their dinners and started in eating like —ha ha—ranch hands. The food was only slightly chilled; the warm stoneware plates had kept the food from getting too cold.

"Yeah, if I do stay here while I'm taking classes I might need a larger one. I can use my laptop on that one but a computer and an open school book wouldn't fit."

Beau stopped eating and looked at her like she had two heads.

"What?"

"Well, I was kind of thinking that if you stayed, you would be joining me in my room."

She shook her head. She didn't think it was appropriate for them to be sharing a room in his parents' house.

He continued on, "As my wife."

She choked on the drink of iced tea she'd just taken. When she stopped sputtering, she said with a squeak, "Your wife?"

He nodded and looked completely serious.

"Beau, are you seriously asking me to marry you over lukewarm meatloaf and mashed potatoes, in my room, while I'm in my pajamas?"

"Oh, well I didn't think—I mean, um—I can come up with a better plan, or um…."

Wasn't he cute all flustered? Her heart expanded, filling her whole chest like it was going to burst. Yep, this was true love alright. "Yes."

"Yes?"

"Yes, I'll marry you."

"Really? Even though I fucked up the proposal with no flowers or a ring or a fancy night out?"

"Yes, but you better come up with a ring and a fancy night out or something other than a backhanded proposal to tell your family and mine," she said with a huff. But she didn't think he was listening because he'd put down his fork, moved the table to the side, pushed her back on the bed, and was kissing her like there was no tomorrow. And that was just fine with her.

When he stopped to breathe he whispered, "I love you Alyssa. From the first moment you stepped on this ranch I wanted you. But over the weeks you've been here, that wanting has turned to love, admiration, and respect. You're beautiful to look at, which is all I saw at first. But your beauty is not only skin deep, it's soul deep. Over the last few months I've fallen head over heels in love with you. You saying you'll marry me has made me the happiest man in Colorado—maybe the whole world."

"I love you too, Beau. I didn't like you very much that first day, but I did think you were sexy. Since then, I've seen your real character, and I will be happy to mesh my life with yours. We might have to go to Washington once in a while to see my dad and help with his breeding program. In fact, I'm sure he'll want strong assurances that we'll go visit or he might not give his blessing. And he'll want to see any grand-children we might produce."

Beau laughed. "Not a problem, sweetheart. We don't have to be tied to this ranch twenty-four-seven. We've got plenty of other workers to be able to take time off to go see your dad. And it might be fun to have two separate herds to exper-iment with, to see if my ideas, and yours, work over multiple herds."

"Good. Now, enough of the talking, already. Kiss me, Beau."

"Gladly."

They eventually finished most of their dinner, putting

their cold meatloaf into the rolls and turning them into sandwiches. The iced tea was watered down and warm, but the brownies were perfect, as was the joy they had in thoughts of the future.

CHAPTER 32

*A*lyssa woke up alone, which sucked, but Beau had left her a note saying a neighboring ranch had asked if he could come over and give them a hand. He'd see her later when he finished. She couldn't fault him for helping a neighbor, but she'd wanted to talk to him about what to tell his family and hers. And she was a little surprised she hadn't heard him talking to the neighbor. She supposed the discussion could wait until later, but she was bursting with excitement to tell everyone.

The only one in the kitchen was the old yellow lab that was living out his golden years in the house after having been a working dog his whole life. His tail hit the floor a couple of times when she walked in and then he went back to sleep. Alyssa smiled, remembering some of the animals her dad had allowed to live in the house over the years. Most of them had been old or in some other way handicapped, and unable to work and live outdoors.

She was just finished eating when Cade and Chase came in from outside.

"Alyssa. Good, you're up. Can you come with us out to the

pasture? One of the hired hands mentioned a heifer and her calf that needed to be looked at," Cade said.

She went on full alert. "Of course, what did he say was the problem?"

Cade looked at Chase then back at her. "Oh, um, nothing of huge significance. He thought the calf wasn't nursing too well."

"Alright. I'm done here, so let's go."

Chase cleared his throat. "We were kind of thinking about taking some horses out rather than the truck. Since it's not an emergency and it's a nice day."

Cade nodded. "Yeah, let's take some sandwiches with us, in case it takes us a while."

Alyssa frowned. That didn't sound like a normal plan. "Sandwiches? Horses? That doesn't sound very expedient."

Cade grinned. "No, but it sounds like a whole lot more fun, don't you think? You haven't had much fun since you got here—we've only taken the horses out a couple of times. Come on, don't you miss riding?"

"I do but…."

"No buts. Let's get some grub together and head out to check on the cattle and have a picnic. We'll have our phones and if anyone needs us, they can bring a truck out."

She still thought it sounded odd, but she would like to get on a horse. They'd been too busy during calving season for riding. "Okay, you've won me over."

"Good, you get some supplies into a saddle bag and we'll get some food ready. We already saddled the horses."

She laughed at their audacity and went out to load up a saddle bag with whatever they might need out in the pasture.

They spent the whole day searching for the elusive heifer and calf, only to find out late in the afternoon that the hired hand had brought the troublesome pair into the calving barn and Beau had looked at him when he got back from the neighbor's. She'd enjoyed the ride and the picnic but was ready to head back and see Beau. They had spotted a couple of cattle she'd taken a closer look at. One looked like had tangled with some barbed wire. She hadn't needed stitches, but Alyssa had cleaned the wound and put some salve on it. She needed to record her findings in the database later. They brushed down the horses and gave them food and water for the evening. The twins said they had one more job before they came into the house, so they would see her at dinner.

Meg met her at the back door. "Alyssa, I forgot to tell you, we're having company tonight. We're going to eat in the formal dining room. You might want to put on a nice dress for the occasion."

Alyssa nodded, but all she really wanted to do was see Beau for five minutes.

"We'll be eating in about forty-five minutes, so you've got time to shower and change."

Well, hell. That shot seeing Beau right in the foot. She barely had time to clean up and be downstairs. She wondered who the company was, that was worthy of a dress. They'd had neighbors drop by from time to time and they'd used the dining room, but they'd not dressed up past good jeans and a nice blouse. She did have some dresses with her for church or school parties. She'd had to bring everything with her when she'd come to the Rockin' K so her roommates could find someone to share the rent with.

She finished in thirty-eight minutes and went by Beau's room to see if they could have five minutes together, before the dinner, but he wasn't there. She stuffed her disappointment down and headed for the dining room. She didn't hear the normal chatter of the family entertaining guests. Maybe they hadn't arrived yet.

When she walked into the dining room, she knew she'd been had. There were bouquets of roses on every flat surface.

A large screen TV sat at one end of the table, and on that TV was her entire family and Rachel. They were all grinning at her. She looked at the Kipling family and they were all grinning too. No one said one word. Finally, she found Beau off to one side of the room and lifted an eyebrow at him.

He approached her and got down on one knee. "Alyssa Jefferson, will you do me the very great honor of becoming my wife?"

She laughed and said, "Yes, Beauregard Kipling, I will marry you—providing Daddy didn't tell you no." She turned her head toward the TV and camera perched on top of it.

Hank laughed. "Nope, the boy gave me an excellent spiel and I gave him my blessing."

"He scared me for a minute before he finally consented." Beau shuddered dramatically. "I never talked so much or so fast in my life. He just sat there not saying a word."

She laughed. "That's my daddy, a man of few words."

"You could have warned me." Beau fished a ring box out of his pocket and held it out to her.

She gasped. How had he found the time to get her a ring after spending half the day at the neighbor's ranch? She narrowed her eyes at him. "You didn't go to a neighbor's ranch, did you. You lied to me. Again."

Beau looked wide-eyed and a little nervous.

Hank groaned. "Alyssa, for God's sake, cut the man some slack. He wanted to surprise you."

She pointed at the twins. "And you guys were decoys."

They grinned back at her. "Guilty as charged."

She shook her head at them and then laughed.

Tony said, "Mama? What's Uncle B doing on the floor? Does he want to play trucks with Lyssa?"

Emma laughed. With tears in her eyes, she said. "Uncle Beau is asking Alyssa to marry him, so she can be your Aunt Alyssa."

"Yay, Aunt Lyssa." He clapped his hands and then turned back to his mother. "Mama? What's an aunt? Not a tiny bug?"

"It's like an uncle only it's a girl. Now shush, baby, so she can look at the ring. We'll talk about it later."

Alyssa grinned at Emma and opened the ring box and there was the most beautiful ring she'd ever seen. It had a main diamond set low, so it wouldn't catch on anything and there were three tiny rubies, channel set into the band, on each side of the diamond. "Beau, it's gorgeous. I love it."

Beau breathed a sigh of relief that was loud enough that everyone heard it and started laughing. He put the ring on her finger and it fit perfectly. He finally stood up and she flew into his arms to kiss him silly.

Rachel said, "Enough kissing already. I want to see the ring."

Hank said, "Bless you, Rachel."

Alyssa kissed Beau one last time and then turned to show her family, best friend, and her new family-to-be the ring. Pandemonium broke out as congratulations were given. Champagne was opened, and toasts were made to the new couple.

Rachel pointed. "Look."

Hank shook his head. "Well, I'll be damned."

Alyssa looked at the stunned expressions of her entire family and demanded, "What is it?"

Hank picked up the laptop and turned it, the room swimming past. He turned it toward the window and walked nearer to it.

Alyssa gasped. There, in the window, was the town peacock in full array. She burst into tears while the Jeffersons cheered and the Kiplings looked confused.

Rachel took pity on them and explained. "The peacock has a reputation of showing up and giving his approval or blessing at whatever might be going on at the time."

Hank said, in awe, "He's never been out to the ranch in all the years I've lived here, until today."

Alyssa laughed through her tears. "Even the town peacock is giving his approval."

Both families laughed and marveled at the sight—except Adam who looked skeptical.

When all the commotion died down, Beau took her in his arms and whispered, "Better?"

She smiled up at him. "Perfect."

The End

ACKNOWLEDGMENTS

This book is a direct result from a conversation I had with my daughter, Sarah. She said, "Mom if you want to write a cowboy series and everyone already loves Alyssa from The Rancher's Lady then make your first book about her."

A light bulb moment for sure. I hope you love reading it as much as I loved writing it.

My brother, Tim, answered many questions about calving season and read the book in it's very rough form to make sure I got the facts straight. Any errors are mine not his. My friend, Ronlyn, also read it in it's rough form to ensure I had the correct information without being too gory for a romance novel. Birth in humans or animals is not a clean, pretty event. My kids, Jonathan and Sarah, and their spouses listened to much rambling and gave me very good advice, often! My grand-daughters share their joy for life and give me lots of fodder for the children in my books.

ABOUT THE AUTHOR

I am a former techy turned writer. I'm writing two small town contemporary romance series with some other ideas percolating in my brain. The Lake Chelan Series is the first series and there are several more books planned for it. The Burlap and Barbed Wire series is a spinoff from the Lake Chelan series. All the books are stand alone but they are also fun to read in order.

I have lived in Colorado, Hawaii, and currently Washington. I'm a member of RWA (Romance Writers of America) and the local chapters GSRWA (Greater Seattle RWA) and Eastside RWA.

My family consists of two grown children, their spouses, two adorable grand-daughters, and one grand dog. I started reading at a young age with the Nancy Drew mysteries and have continued to be an avid reader. My favorite reading material these days is romance in most of the genres.

My favorite activity is playing with my grand-daughters!

Some of the jobs I have held are a carnation grower's worker, a trap club puller, a pizza hut waitress, a software engineer, an international trainer, and a business program manager.

And for something really unusual... I once had a raccoon as a pet.

~

To sign up for Shirley's New Release Newsletter, send email to shirleypenick@outlook.com, Subject: Newsletter.

For more information:
www.shirleypenick.com

CPSIA information can be obtained
at www.ICGtesting.com
Printed in the USA
LVHW082327060619
620472LV00031B/552/P

9 781984 012265